To David, whose imagination inspired me to write.
If you can dream it, you can be it.

TABLE OF CONTENTS

1 * A CRY FOR HELP

"Can I stay up and read for a little while, Mom?" pleaded David. His mom smiled and handed David a book. She adjusted the lights in the room so that he could read, gave him a kiss and left the room. David began reading, straining to avoid sleep. He knew that as soon as he fell asleep, the nightmare would begin again. But soon, his eyelids grew heavy. Suddenly, as if a black curtain had dropped over his eyes, the dream began.

The sound of his own heart grew louder in his ears. Its steady thump lulled him into a deeper sleep; but just as his breathing slowed, the black curtain in front of him lifted, revealing the back of what appeared to be a very tall, very large man. Long white hair cascaded down his back, almost to his waist. The man was wearing a dark gray robe, tied in the middle, with billowing sleeves that hinted at massive arms. Swirling glitter floated up and down in an endless, mesmerizing dance around him. Dark streamers of smoke wafted across the sky.

The thumping of David's heart grew louder and faster as the figure began to turn. Then a voice filled David's head, drowning out the beating of his heart. The voice was deep and gravelly, almost a growl. "I can feel your fear. It fills me. Soon, I will be the true master of dreams and all will tremble before me."

David began to sweat. The dream continued.

David didn't want to look but he couldn't turn away. As the figure spoke, he finished turning towards David. David flinched as the full face appeared. The creature's skin was gray and shiny, with a high forehead topped by white hair that was swept straight back and caught the light of the glitter that continued swirling around. Its nose and mouth were set in a smooth muzzle that jutted slightly from the face. The nostrils were large and black, and flared as the creature exhaled. The ears were small and round, set close to the head but slightly higher than David was used to seeing. Its eyes were closed and it seemed to be meditating. There was a slight smile on its face.

As David gazed at the creature, he noticed that its massive hands held a cylindrical piece of glass mounted on a wooden rod with a gold handle. The glass revolved slowly, reflecting a rainbow of colors, seemingly pulled from the glittering air. A wisp of dark smoke wafted up from the glass.

David was so fascinated with the scene that he forgot to be scared. But this sense of calm was suddenly shattered when the eyes of the creature snapped open. If David had been awake, he would have screamed. The eyes were black. Completely black. Dark pools looked like empty eye sockets, but David could see a shiny film covering the eyes and could feel them boring right into his head. The thumping of his heart returned and now it was beating a rapid staccato.

David could see the reflection of light against dazzling white canine teeth. The growling voice continued, "No one can help you. He can't help you. He is lost forever. Wizard or not, he can't escape his fate. The world is mine to control." With a swirl of gray, and a tumble of glitter, the figure whirled and the curtain of black returned.

David woke up, shivering and damp. "Daddy! Mommy!" he yelled in panic. A few minutes later his dad arrived looking rumpled and tired. "Dad, I had the dream again. And it seemed so real this time!"

His dad sat on the edge of the bed and stroked his son's hair as David told him about the dream. "Why do I keep having these dreams, Daddy? Is there something wrong with me?"

"No, there's nothing wrong with you, and you aren't alone," his dad replied. "There was an article in the newspaper today talking about an epidemic of bad dreams. It seems people around the world are having a rash of nightmares. Here, let me get it." He retrieved the article and handed it to David.

Worldwide Complaints of Nightmares and Restlessness

Sleep specialists around the world are puzzled by the rapid rise in patients who report that they are having trouble sleeping, and that when they do get to sleep their dreams are more likely to be characterized as nightmares. Dr. Red Knight, of the North American Sleep Institute, believes that the answer lies in the way people view the world situation. "When the world is at peace people sleep soundly, but when there are troubles in the world, like the recent terrorist attacks and war, then people become nervous and jumpy, and their sleep patterns are disrupted."

Others attribute the strange dream states to less scientific solutions, like unhappy spirits, retribution from God for perceived misdeeds, or even the work of the devil.

The studies done so far indicate that children are encountering this problem in much larger numbers than adults. Dr. Knight believes that the reason for this is that "Children are highly imaginative and this ability to suspend disbelief and conjure all sorts of incredible visions magnifies the problem."

Dr. Knight said, "We continue to search for answers and right now we ask everybody to curl up with a good book, drink some hot chocolate, listen to some of your favorite music, or take a warm bath before bed. Anything that relaxes you will help you sleep."

David glanced up from the article as he finished reading it. Instead of being relieved to find that others were experiencing the same thing, he was deeply troubled by the idea that nightmares and sleeplessness were common all over the world. "Dad, are there really evil spirits? Have I done something wrong to cause my bad dreams?"

David's dad sighed. "David, the whole idea of evil spirits is an attempt to describe something that can't be explained using science. Many years ago, when people who were sick acted strange, evil spirits were blamed because doctors couldn't figure out what was wrong with them. There is probably a scientific, logical explanation for this. Doctors just haven't found it yet."

He tousled his son's hair. "Now go back to sleep. Don't forget we're collecting Monarch butterfly eggs in the morning!" He straightened the covers and tucked David back in, then returned to his own bed to try to get another hour of sleep.

As the sun rose, so did David's spirits. He forgot about his nightmare in the excitement of the expedition to hunt for Monarch eggs. For the second year in a row, he and his parents would be observing the whole cycle of life, from egg to caterpillar to chrysalis and then to butterfly. This year they were going to tag the butterflies that would migrate south to Mexico.

They walked through a field near their house, searching for the milkweed plants that represented the sole food source for the monarch caterpillar. David was a tall, thin boy with light brown hair. He was constantly in motion and today was no exception. As the family looked at the leaves, he danced and jumped around, humming to himself and trying to absorb all the things that he could see. His eyes were striking. Light blue with flecks of green, they were always moving, examining the surrounding world, trying to take it all in.

David's father looked up as a brilliant orange butterfly suddenly fluttered in front of his face. "David, look!" he whispered excitedly and together they watched as the butterfly hovered over the nearby plants and then settled on the bottom of a leaf. They waited in silence until the butterfly moved to other plants and then ran over to inspect the leaf. David saw it right away—a tiny football shaped white egg attached to the bottom of the leaf.

"We found one!" David shouted and together they removed the leaf from the plant and placed it in the plastic bowl they had brought, on top of a damp paper towel. They continued to look at leaves, and in a very short time had collected several more eggs.

As they walked home, David's parents had to run to catch up with him. He was bouncing from toe to toe and spinning in a circle waiting to cross the street to continue the journey home.

Back at the house, they carefully placed the leaves in an empty pretzel barrel. As evening approached, David again began to dread going to bed. He thought that maybe if he concentrated hard enough he could stop time, but sadly no power in the world could do that. All too soon it was time to go to sleep, and once again the black curtain dropped. Again, he heard his heart beating and again the strange creature with the black eyes appeared. The black eyes were pools of darkness. David hated darkness. As David watched, the black eyes grew larger and larger until they enveloped David and he was falling, falling through darkness, drowning in it. He woke up to darkness. The lights were out and the room was pitch black. Shivering uncontrollably, David fumbled for the lamp until he finally found the knob and turned it on, flooding the room with light.

He rubbed the sleep out of his eyes and thought about what he had seen. It wasn't real. It seemed real but he had never seen anything like that, so he knew it was only a dream. But what did it mean? He climbed out of bed, wrapped a blanket around himself and sat on the floor of his room thinking hard.

"Help me."

David jerked his head up and looked around. There was no one there. David's cat, Cutie skidded suddenly into the room. David smiled. "Did you say that?"

The gray striped tabby cat stared and meowed loudly. David giggled. "Well if what I heard was, 'Feed me,' then I would think it was you. I must have imagined it."

By this time the early morning sun was beginning to peek in through the window. David stood up and headed for the kitchen with Cutie rubbing against his leg and meowing the whole way. As soon as he opened the cat food can, the meowing grew louder and more desperate. "You would think that we

11

never feed you." He dumped the food into two bowls and ruffled the fur on Cutie's head as the cat began gobbling the morsels. A gray and white cat suddenly appeared in the doorway. He didn't make a sound but strolled slowly to the other bowl, sniffed it with disdain, and walked away with his tail in the air. David laughed at how different the two cats were. "Spud, you'd better eat up because Cutie will eat all your food too."

As David left the kitchen, he passed the big plastic pretzel barrel that contained the milkweed leaves and Monarch butterfly eggs. He stopped to examine the eggs. One had a black spot on top, which indicated that it would hatch soon. That one must have been laid earlier. The black spot was the tiny caterpillar developing inside, too small to see without a microscope. Soon he would be able to watch the transformation of caterpillar to butterfly again. It was something he never tired of seeing.

As he headed back toward his room, he heard it again: "Help me."

This time the voice was louder. It had a gravelly quality to it but it was not the voice from his dream. This voice sounded muffled. David shook his head and looked around. He didn't see anyone. The nightmare must be affecting his mind.

He decided to watch some TV to help him forget the nightmare and the strange voice, and soon he was able to relax and enjoy mindless entertainment.

The day went by quickly. David played with his friends, creating an imaginary game in which he was the wizard who had to save the world from the bad guy. Later, he had a wrestle fight with his dad, which like all their wrestle fights, turned into a complicated scenario involving magic and imaginary weapons.

All too soon, evening approached. As David was getting ready for bed, he heard it again.

"Help me."

He looked around but didn't see anyone except his dad, sitting in the recliner with his nose buried in the newspaper. The voice definitely hadn't been his dad's voice.

Even though David dreaded going to sleep, he soon

found himself in bed again with heavy eyes. This time when he woke up he didn't remember his dream. He wasn't even sure he had been dreaming at all. He stumbled out of bed and began the cat feeding ritual again.

When lunchtime arrived, David noticed that one of the white eggs was gone. He picked up the leaf and looked underneath it. Scooting around on the underside of the leaf was a tiny caterpillar. "Mom, Dad, we've got our first caterpillar!"

They all looked at the caterpillar under a microscope. David's parents exchanged worried glances as they looked at the tiny wriggling insect. His father muttered, "Something's wrong. It doesn't look right and those funny brown spots around the middle look like tumors. I don't think this one's going to make it." David's mother agreed, but David wanted to believe that it would be OK.

Another afternoon flew by and soon the sun was setting, bringing an eerie silence to the house. As bedtime approached, David suddenly heard it again.

"Help me."

This time the voice was clear and insistent. David glanced around his room and then wandered into the dining room.

"Help me!"

The voice was so loud now that David was sure his parents could hear it too, but they seemed totally oblivious to the sound. David headed for his room to try and escape the voice and that's when it suddenly dawned on him to look at the caterpillars. One of them was perched on a leaf, standing almost straight up with tiny front feet against the plastic. David stared at the caterpillar, which began to shake violently.

"Can you hear me? Please tell me you can hear me!"

David glanced at his mother and father, leaned close to the plastic and whispered, "Yes, I can hear you. Who are you?"

The effect on the caterpillar was electric. David could have sworn that the little worm did a complete somersault. Then it settled down and said, "I'm a little wizard in big trouble."

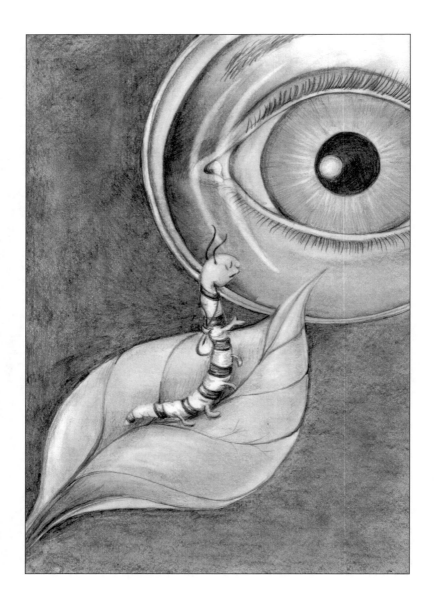

2 ＊ THE WIZARD'S TALE

"I need your help!" David glanced over at his parents who were busy chatting about the day's events at the dining room table. He should have been astounded. David had always wanted to believe that there was real magic in the world, but up until two minutes ago, the only magic he had ever seen involved illusions and sleight-of-hand by experienced magicians. Two minutes ago, real magic existed only in the imaginary realm inside his head. Now, everything he had believed before appeared to be wrong.

He should have been astounded, but he wasn't. David readily accepted the fact that a tiny caterpillar, no bigger than a grain of rice, had just spoken to him and proclaimed that he was a wizard in trouble.

David reached into the pretzel barrel, extracted the leaf with the caterpillar on it and ran into his bedroom. His parents glanced questioningly after his retreating figure but then went back to their discussion.

David set down the leaf with the caterpillar. He rummaged around in his closet and emerged holding his magnifying glass. He picked up the leaf and peered down through the magnifying glass at the little caterpillar. It promptly stood up, or at least made an attempt that looked like someone standing up. Over half of the caterpillar's body arched upward off the leaf so that the little guy resembled the letter "L." He wasn't sure what the next step should be so he waited and watched.

The caterpillar's mandibles now moved and David heard the voice again, "I thank you for hearing my plea and beg you to listen to my story."

Just then David heard the scrape of a chair as his mother got up from the table. He panicked, knowing that she would be coming in soon to tell him to get ready for bed. Somehow, he didn't think his parents would understand. He jerked open the drawer of his nightstand, removed a plastic spell wand and put it on top of the nightstand. He then placed the leaf and magnifying glass in the drawer and closed it. As he slid it shut, he whispered to the caterpillar, "I'll be back soon."

David called to his mom, "I'm getting ready for bed, Mom." He retreated to the bathroom, washed up, and brushed his teeth. His mother came in to tuck him into bed. She saw the plastic wand on the nightstand and went to put it away in the drawer where the leaf and the caterpillar were hidden, but David intervened. "Wait, I don't want the wand in the drawer tonight. I'm going to be a wizard in my dreams and I'll need a wand, so I want to sleep with it . . . please!" His mom laughed, handed the wand to him and warned, "Don't let the evil wizards win."

"I won't, Mom. You know that Magical David always wins." He snuggled under the covers and his mom adjusted the lights.

She looked at him again, and then gave him a light kiss. "Sleep tight." She left the bedroom door slightly ajar.

David jumped up and retrieved the leaf and the magnifying glass from the drawer. He whispered, "Who are you?"

The caterpillar began speaking rapidly as if it was afraid it would lose this chance to tell its story. "My name is Houdin. I am . . . I mean, I was . . . the master wizard in a place called Remin."

David couldn't help interrupting, "Remin? I've never heard of that. Can I find it on my globe in the morning?"

Houdin made a noise that sounded like a chuckle, "No, you won't find it on any map or globe. It's hard to explain but I'll do my best." Houdin paused as if trying to decide the best way to continue the story. "When you dream, does it seem real?"

David pondered for a moment and then said, "Sometimes...well most of the time..."

Houdin now began speaking like a teacher giving a lecture. "Dreams are the brain's way of organizing information. In order to do that, images are processed but the brain has trouble distinguishing these pictures from the ones you see while you are awake."

David interrupted again, "What does this have to do with your problem?" He wanted to listen to the story but each sentence brought up more questions in his mind. He constantly raced ahead of the story, thinking, imagining, and planning, using every tidbit of information that he heard as a springboard to adventure.

Houdin sighed. "It has everything to do with Remin. Remin is a different world than your world."

David couldn't stop himself. "Wow! I've always read about other worlds: worlds behind mirrors, worlds where scarecrows are kings, worlds with schools of magic. Now you're telling me that other worlds really exist?"

Houdin could barely contain his annoyance at being interrupted again, but he realized that this was all too new to David and he really shouldn't begrudge the boy his inquisitiveness. "I don't know about other worlds, but Remin exists alongside your world and provides an important service. When you dream, the threads of that dream travel through Remin where the imaginary aspects of the dream are given the illusion of reality. Without Remin, dreams would be like comic books. The brain wouldn't be able to process the images correctly and everyone in your world would be affected. It's hard to explain but that's the best I can do right now." Houdin paused to allow David time to think about this piece of the puzzle.

David's eyes had widened as the story unfolded. The idea that there was some other place involved in his dreams was exciting and scary at the same time. He was just getting ready to ask his next question when he heard a noise in the hallway. His mother was coming to check on him. He suddenly realized that he hadn't planned for this part of the evening very well. He should have had a book prepared so that he could have been reading it when his mother came in. He would have to improvise. In the three seconds that it took for his mother to reach his door, he slid the magnifying glass under his covers, placed the leaf into the drawer and grabbed a plastic building toy from his nightstand. The door swung open and his mother stepped into the room.

"All right, it's time to . . ." Her voice trailed off. She had expected to find her son reading in bed again. Instead he was sitting up in bed, holding one of his plastic toys that he had constructed into some kind of imaginary machine. David looked at her and laughed, "I was just making up a story to go with my new machine. Do you want me to tell you all about it?"

David was counting on the fact that this was not the time and place for a long, convoluted, imaginary story, and he was right. His mother took a step back, smiled and quickly said, "Tell me tomorrow. It's time for bed. Turn out the light, please."

David frowned. He started to argue, then stopped, turned out the lights and rolled over, pretending to go to sleep. His mother kissed him on the cheek and left the room, leaving the door partway open.

He lay there in the dark, listening for the sounds coming from the other rooms of the house. While he waited for his parents to go to bed, he thought about what Houdin had said. A place that manipulated dreams. It sounded unbelievable, but then again, he was having intelligent conversations with a caterpillar, so maybe it wasn't as unbelievable as it seemed. He wondered if the dream about the man with the dark eyes had anything to do with Houdin, or Remin, or if it was just his brain trying to organize his thoughts. He thought about Houdin. Maybe everyone in Remin looked like little caterpillars. That would mean that the man with the dark eyes was not part of

Houdin's problem. Maybe Houdin could explain it. He would have to ask when Houdin's story was finished.

Finally, he heard his dad turn off the TV. Now the only sound was the constant keyboard clicking that told him his mother was still up and working at the computer, but soon he heard her feeding the cats and knew that she was headed for bed. Sure enough, silence followed soon afterwards.

He waited another couple of minutes and then rolled over and turned on his nightstand light. He retrieved the magnifying glass from under the covers and pulled the leaf out of the nightstand drawer. The caterpillar was gone!

He turned the leaf over a couple of times, but nothing was there. He looked in the drawer but could not see his tiny visitor. He grew more frantic with every passing moment. Suddenly he spied a tiny speck moving across his pillow. A quick look with the magnifying glass confirmed that he had found the little wizard again. He propped himself up on his elbows and whispered, "Why did you do that? I thought I squished you or lost you."

Houdin stopped his march across the pillow and said, "I can't miss this opportunity. I've had to shout for you to hear me but I can't keep shouting like this. Please lie down."

It sounded like a strange request but there was nothing normal about this night so far, so David rolled over and placed his head on the pillow next to Houdin. He waited and suddenly felt a tickling sensation on his ear. Houdin was crawling right into his ear! David giggled but tried to keep his head still. Suddenly, it all became clear when Houdin began speaking again. Now the voice was quieter and more controlled and David could hear him quite clearly.

"I really need your help. If you can hear me clearly, please nod."

David nodded his head once in an exaggerated motion and whispered, "Yes, I can hear you." He paused, waiting for Houdin to continue.

"Good, this is the first bit of luck I have had since this awful curse was placed on me. Now let me . . ."

"Curse? What curse?" David couldn't help himself.

Houdin replied dryly, "If you would let me finish my story, I might answer all your questions."

"Sorry," David said sheepishly.

Houdin continued, "I am under a reincarnation curse. I . . ."

Before David could stop himself, he interrupted again, "You mean you aren't a caterpillar?"

"Of course not! But you couldn't know that."

"Let me start at the beginning. In Remin, there are certain people who have the innate ability to manipulate dreams. We call them dreamweavers, or just weavers. The weavers rely on a device called the Imaginator to provide power for their manipulations."

"A man named Thane was one of the dreamweavers. He found that he liked working with dreams that were dark and scary. You would call them nightmares. Anyway, Thane began working exclusively with nightmare threads."

"In spite of his affinity for the dark, Thane was an idealist. He thought he knew what was best. He stole the Imaginator in a misguided attempt to help Remin. However, he became intoxicated by the power and craved more. He decided that he wanted to control the dreams of everyone in your world and he wanted those dreams to be nightmares."

"Several attempts were made to retrieve the Imaginator but they all failed. I led the last attempt and almost succeeded. I tracked Thane down and confronted him. I tried to get him to see reason but he was so hungry for power that either he didn't see or didn't care that his actions were destroying Remin. Thane got the better of me at the last moment and was able to successfully perform the reincarnation curse, although for the life of me I can't figure out how he did it. I am now stuck in an endless cycle of egg, caterpillar, chrysalis, and butterfly. I live, I die, and I wake up to find myself in an egg again—each time in a new place. I've lost count of how many times I have now been through this cycle!"

"How can you break the curse? What does Thane look like? What did you look like before Thane cursed you? How do you get to Remin? What . . ."

"Whoa, slow down. I'll answer as well as I can," Houdin interrupted. He liked the fact that David was eager and enthusiastic to help, but had a lot of reservations about how much help he could expect from a child. There was something promising about this boy; after all, he was the only one in all the reincarnations that had ever heard Houdin. But still, he was young. Oh well, he thought; when you're a caterpillar, stuck in another world, you can't be picky. "The only way I know to break this type of curse is to disrupt the power of the one who placed the curse—in this case Thane. I'm not sure how to do that. Thane obviously still lives, because I am still under the curse. Assuming that he still controls the Imaginator, his power must have increased since I last saw him."

Suddenly Houdin felt like he was spinning. David had suddenly sat up in bed and Houdin was now upside down inside an ear. David sounded like he was shouting in his excitement. "Are you telling me that Thane is causing my nightmares? What does he look like?"

Houdin scrambled around to right himself and said, "Thane? I don't know. Tall, long white hair, kind of bear-like from your perspective. Not too different from me when I'm my old self, except for his eyes. Thane's eyes are pitch black. I didn't remember him that way, but when I caught up with him the last time, it was a little scary to see eyes that were that black." Houdin's voice trailed off. He didn't want to lie but he also didn't want to discourage the one big chance he had to try and get out of the mess he was in. But, David didn't seem discouraged at all. In fact, Thane's description seemed to make the boy positively giddy.

"Tell me what I can do to help. I don't like the nightmares I'm having and it appears that I'm not the only one. People all over the world are having nightmares."

Houdin was startled. "What do you mean?"

21

David retrieved the article that he had just read and repeated it to Houdin. Soon he could hear Houdin muttering to himself and his ear started tickling again because the wizard was now pacing back and forth. "It's worse than I thought. I had hoped that someone else in Remin would have succeeded in recovering the Imaginator by now but that doesn't appear to be the case. That means that Thane's power must be enormous by now. I'm not even sure how long I've been gone." The voice trailed off and the silence lasted so long that David began to think that something was really wrong.

"Houdin?" David had settled back down on the bed.

Another pause and then Houdin's voice came back. He sounded older and more tired. "If nothing has changed since I left Remin then Thane has been in control the whole time. There is no telling how bad things have gotten, both here in your world and in Remin. The nightmares you describe all point to Thane, and Remin has been in trouble longer than your world."

David asked, "How could that be? If my world has seen an increase in nightmares over the last couple of years, hasn't the same amount of time gone by in Remin?"

"No. Time moves differently in Remin. You know that dreams can last days but when you wake up in the morning, only eight hours have gone by. That's the wonder of Remin time. Remin allows you to experience time speeded up, so that an entire dream that takes place over time can occur in a single night."

"Why don't you just go back to Remin and get your friends to help you?" David was starting to get confused by all the twists and turns of the story but it appeared obvious to him that there wasn't a lot he could do to help Houdin.

"I can't," Houdin sighed, "I've tried, but I ran into a little problem."

"What kind of problem?"

"I have the means to get back with me, but because of my form right now I can't perform the spell that will get me back. I need to place spectrum, which I carry with me, on my eyelids. Unfortunately, I DON'T HAVE ANY EYELIDS!"

It was almost funny. David started to laugh but quickly stifled it as he realized the terrible frustration that Houdin must be feeling. Suddenly he had an idea. "I have eyelids. Can you use mine?"

If Houdin had had eyelids, his eyes would have popped wide open. "That's brilliant. Yes, I think that will work. Would you be willing to go to Remin and help me?"

His world turned upside down again as David leaped out of bed and began quickly and quietly throwing on some clothes: a pair of silvery gray pants with many pockets, a pair of black sandals with a spider-web pattern and a gray sweatshirt with a ghostly cartoon decal. The two cats, Spud and Cutie, ambled into the room to see what all the commotion was about. Houdin was excited too. He was muttering to himself and struggling to stay oriented as David's head moved back and forth with the action of getting dressed.

"This just might work."

Suddenly David stopped. "I can't go. My parents won't understand. They'll miss me. I can't hurt them by just disappearing. I'm sorry Houdin."

"Don't worry. I told you that time is different in Remin and I can get us to Remin and back again before morning. Trust me."

David relaxed slightly. Maybe that would work. He had to hope that his parents wouldn't check on him until morning. If they came upstairs and found his bed empty, things would be really bad. He decided to chance it, but maybe it would be better if he left a note. He grabbed a piece of paper out of his composition book and laboriously wrote a note.

As he wrote, he could hear Houdin talking impatiently, "Hurry up, hurry up, what's taking so long?"

David tried to ignore the insistent whine buzzing through his head. He finished the note and put it on his pillow. The note said:

Mom and Dad,
Don't worry. I'm helping a friend. Be back soon.
I love you. David

David had one last request. "I'm ready. I'm trusting you, Houdin. Promise me that if anything happens, you will find some way to let my parents know the whole story. I don't want them to lose me and never find out where I went or what I did."

Houdin hesitated. There was some danger involved in this undertaking and he felt some responsibility for the boy but he knew of no other way to return to Remin. The risk from his viewpoint was worth it. Nevertheless he knew that David was right. David couldn't just disappear and leave his parents without any idea of what happened to him. Houdin couldn't do it, especially not in his present form, but he knew someone who could.

"Yes, I promise. Your parents will be informed of what happens, but you'll have to help me. Can you fill a sink or a tub with water?"

"Yes, I can." He quietly left his room and stepped into the bathroom. He placed the stopper in the tub and added some water. Houdin now asked to be held out over the water. David held him out over the water and saw a few sprinkles of glitter fall to the water. He didn't understand what he was seeing but Houdin seemed satisfied. They both moved back into the bedroom. David grabbed his jacket from the closet door and put it on. He didn't know what the weather would be like in Remin, but he thought he'd better be prepared.

"OK Houdin, what do I have to do?"

"Lie down again so I can get on the bed."

As soon as Houdin was on the bed, David looked again with the magnifying glass. Houdin was standing on his back prolegs and was using his front, or true legs, to struggle with the brown spots that David and his parents had seen earlier. David suddenly realized that they weren't tumors—they were leather bags. The legs dipped into the bags and a sprinkle of what looked like glitter began to cascade down Houdin's body.

Houdin began shouting again, "This is spectrum. It harnesses the power of the Imaginator and will allow us to get to Remin. Pick me up on your finger and put me near your eyes."

David placed his finger next to Houdin who climbed on. He lay down at the foot of the bed, closed his eyes and placed his finger next to the bridge of his nose. Soon he felt the light tickling that signaled a caterpillar moving across his face. The tickling stopped in the center of the first eyelid, and then continued until it stopped in the center of the second eyelid. It then returned to the bridge of his nose.

Houdin must have been surveying his handiwork because he exclaimed, "Yes, that's perfect. The spectrum is on both eyelids. Are you ready David?"

Houdin moved back across David's face and settled again in his right ear. David waited and then heard, "Saleemia." The room began to spin (or maybe it was David that began to spin). He couldn't tell. His eyes were squeezed shut and his hands were clenched tightly at his sides. If his eyes had been open, he would have seen a vortex of clouds open underneath him that seemed to go right through his bed. David and the little hitchhiking wizard tumbled through the vortex and vanished, leaving behind an empty room and two very puzzled cats.

3 * RAINBOW POWER

If you have ever been in a vortex between worlds, you know what happened next. David, who was experiencing a vortex for the first time, struggled to keep from panicking. He kept his eyes clenched tightly shut, afraid that if he opened them, the spell would be broken or changed. His eyelids felt hot, for as soon as Houdin had uttered the correct spell, the power of the spectrum on his eyelids had ignited and the heat was radiating outward from his body. He felt like he was spinning but at the same time he could feel the familiar softness of blankets against his back. He panted for breath. His heart pounded.

Suddenly everything changed. His bed was no longer there. Something that felt like grass pressed into his back and brushed his cheeks. A crisp breeze washing over him replaced the warm air of his bedroom, and the spinning sensation vanished as if an amusement park ride had come to a quick halt.

Close to the ground, the vortex was closing. Almost the size of a dinner plate, it roiled with misty clouds in the center. Suddenly, two animal shapes, one of them gray and white, leaped through it and scampered across the field.

David opened his eyes and peered around at the rustling sound, but saw only a field of tall corn staring up at a gray, cloudless sky. Tiny black streamers wriggled through the air high over his head. He cautiously sat up. The spell had worked!

He was in Remin! Well, at least, he was somewhere else. It must be Remin, he thought. Houdin's voice suddenly was chattering excitedly in his ear.

"It worked! We're here. I'm back. You did it David. I can't thank you enough. This is more than I could have hoped for when you heard me call for help." David couldn't see it, but Houdin's head was swiveling around trying to get his bearings.

Houdin's next statement took some of the excitement out of the whole adventure. "We should be in Remin City but it appears that we are outside the city. That could be a problem. The door won't recognize you and it can't see me. The spectrum must have weakened after all that time in my sacks, or maybe it's because I don't have a wand to concentrate the power of the spell." He suddenly stopped for he had been talking to himself more than to David. "Oh well, we'll have to make the best of it."

David grinned and looked around. He didn't understand what Houdin meant about the door recognizing him and he was slightly disappointed to find himself standing in what looked like an ordinary field of corn, but the unusual sky above him was enough to put all that out of his mind. Tall rows of corn surrounded him and now he noticed that the air was littered with little glimmers. He held out his hand and one of the glimmers landed on his palm. He stared at it. It looked like one of the spectrum that Houdin had placed on his eyelids, only bigger. It was like a tiny piece of glitter. The difference was that this glitter appeared to be alive. It was a light shade of green yet it was translucent. The color appeared to be pulsing through the tiny object. He captured another one. This one was red but it had the same unique qualities. Like dancing snowflakes, silver and blue glimmers also landed on David's outstretched hands.

"Houdin, what is this stuff you call spectrum? It's in the air."

"Yes, but there should be a lot more of it. Because Thane controls the Imaginator, the volume of spectrum in the air appears to be greatly diminished. This does not bode well for our journey. Assuming that Kira is still alive, it would be better if she explains it to you. She's the Imaginator expert. She can fill us in on what has been going on and possibly give us some assistance in our search for Thane. She was with me when I confronted Thane, so we need to find her as soon as we get into Remin City."

"Where do we go?" asked David, for in looking around, he saw only tall stalks of corn.

"This is the field outside of Remin. If you were a little taller, you could just look over the corn stalks to find the way. You'll have to place me on some of the corn and let me climb up and figure out which way to go," said Houdin. He could see that this journey was going to be a whole series of hardships for a boy and a very weak caterpillar wizard.

David stretched up to place Houdin on a tall stalk of corn and waited while the tiny caterpillar slowly climbed up the stalk. While he waited, he listened to the faint rustle of the breeze through the corn. He also heard a faint "pfffft" down near his feet. He searched the ground and soon discovered what appeared to be a small glass flask-shaped object filled with green and blue spectrum. A few silver spectrum were visible in the mixture as well. As David stared at the vial, a few of the spectrum suddenly spurted out with the "pffft" sound that had attracted his attention in the first place. As the spectrum spiraled back to the ground, they ignited with power and David could see waves of light faintly spreading out from the center of the vial. The ground under the light suddenly dimpled and David reached out and found that the ground was damp. Somehow the spectrum was helping to grow the corn! David had lots of questions for Houdin, or Kira if they could find her.

Soon enough Houdin climbed down the corn stalk. David helped him get back to his ear. "The Remin City gate is just to your left and slightly down a hill."

David turned to his left and began to make his way through the swaying corn. Soon, he came out of the cornfield and saw a large lake. In the center of the lake, he could see an island. The distance was too great to see any details, but the island appeared to be surrounded by a wall, with a few buildings peeking out over the wall. To his right, David saw a path that cut through the field and ended at a stone archway.

Houdin quickly confirmed David's thoughts. "That's Remin City out in the lake and the archway is the only entrance to the city. Let's see if we can convince the door to let you in."

David walked over to the archway. He looked behind him at the path cutting through the cornfield. From here, he could see that the path was actually a road that headed off into the fields until it curved out of sight. The field to the left of the road was full of dead or dying corn stalks. Their dry husks jutted out of the soil, providing a sharp contrast to the healthy stalks across the road waving happily in the brisk air. His ear was tickling as Houdin continually moved around trying to see it all.

Houdin's voice was tinged with deep concern, "Something is very wrong. It looks like they have stopped supplying spectrum to all the fields as if they are trying to conserve their supply. When I was here before, spectrum was everywhere. Thane has most of it now. This is really bad."

David turned from the road and the field and faced the archway. He took a deep breath. He wasn't sure what he had gotten himself into and the adventure so far had been exciting, but it appeared that it was going to get a lot more interesting from here on out. As he stepped around to the front of the archway, he could see that the path sloped downward into the archway, ending at a massive set of purple doors. The doors were set far back in the tunnel of the archway and they should have been in shadow, but instead they blazed with light provided by two torches mounted on either side. David walked down the gently sloping path, his sandals kicking up little puffs of dust as he walked. Obviously, the path wasn't being used very much. Soon enough he stood in front of the doors.

As he came to a stop, the light from the torches dimmed. It looked like the torches were going to go out. They guttered and then suddenly flared into brightness again. David glanced quickly up at the torches and saw a glimmer of red sprinkling onto the torches. The same type of vial he had seen in the cornfield was mounted above each torch although this time it was filled with red spectrum. David marveled at the idea that crops were grown with spectrum and fires stayed lit with spectrum. What other wonders were in store? He was eager for the adventure. Then his excitement sobered as he suddenly realized that if spectrum was so important, and Thane had some kind of control over it, then the world of Remin was in very big trouble. He sighed and readied himself to go on.

The doors were made of wood and were easily 18 feet tall and 12 feet wide. Big enough to drive a truck through, David thought. Two large knotholes were visible, one on each door. Large gold knockers hung down near the center of the doors. Above the door was a gold lettered sign: REMIN CITY.

David walked up to the doors and lifted one of the knockers and let it fall. A resounding clang echoed back at him.

Houdin quickly whispered, "This door leads to a tunnel under the lake. When the door answers, mention my name and see if you can convince the door to let you in."

David waited for someone to come to the door. Suddenly, the two knotholes swiveled to become enormous eyes staring at him. "I don't know you," stated the door flatly. It fell silent.

Swallowing his surprise at being spoken to by the actual door, David replied, "My name is David. I am a friend of Houdin the wizard."

The eyes in the door swiveled to look all around David. "I do not see Houdin." Again the door fell silent.

Not much of a conversationalist, thought David. "Houdin has been transformed into a caterpillar by a curse and is currently sitting in my ear," said David, and even as he said it he realized that it sounded quite silly.

The door stared intently at David for a full minute but then spoke again. "The fact that a worm sits in your ear does not prove your statement. No admittance." The knotholes closed and the door was silent again. No amount of knocking could make it respond again.

Houdin sighed, "I should have known it wouldn't be that easy. That door has always been a little too pig-headed about letting people in. I suppose it's a good thing in a way, but if I ever get back to my old self, I'm going to give that door a piece of my mind."

"This archway is the only entrance into city. The only other way is to attempt to cross the lake and that is not going to be easy. Remin City is well protected and the lake is not going to let you just row on over to the city."

David moved out of the shadow of the archway, up the sloping path, kicking up dust again as he moved out under the open sky. In the distance, he could see a small pier jutting out into the lake. He set off toward the pier at a fast trot. Houdin began talking as soon as it became obvious where they were going. "Remin City is surrounded by Whirlpool Lake. I may be able to aid our passage across the lake using some of the spectrum that I have left but if I am correct and the spectrum's power has been degraded over time, I do not think we can depend on it to insure our safety."

David chuckled, "Well, we'll have to improvise then. If the lake is the only way across, other than that not-so-friendly door, we'll have to take our chances on the lake. Just remember your promise."

If Houdin could have frowned he would have. "I have made a promise and I won't disappoint you, but I don't expect to have to keep it anyway. Hopefully, nothing will happen to you, and at the end of this we'll all live happily ever after. Let's keep a positive outlook, shall we?"

He glanced across the lake at the city. The lake was as smooth as glass. The city was still indistinct because of the distance. A few flags waved in the breeze and a few rooftops were visible but David could see that most of the city was behind a high wall. He was excited to see what the city was like and speeded up the pace.

"Tell me more about this spectrum, Houdin," queried David. "It looks to me like it does more than affect dreams like you mentioned before. I see it everywhere. It's in the air, lying on the ground, and I've also seen a couple of devices that spray it. One was keeping the torches lit in the archway and one was in the cornfield."

Houdin's voice now grew serious. "You're right. Spectrum is the key to life in Remin, both in the city and in the surrounding areas. We use its power to accomplish many things. You already saw that it can keep torches lit to provide light, and to assist in the growing of crops, but spectrum is much more than that."

"There are four main kinds of spectrum. Red spectrum harnesses the power of fire to allow us to control heat. Silver spectrum allows us to control the air around us. We can create breezes and vacuums. Blue spectrum is related to water and green spectrum is the earth power affecting rocks and wood. There are other colors that are produced by the energy of the four main colors. There are small quantities of purple, gold, pink and any other color you can think of. We're still learning what you can do with these specialized spectrum but they all appear to be related to fire, water, air and earth. Each one by itself has a limited usefulness, but by using them in specific combinations we can do wondrous things. Combining green and blue and silver in the cornfield allows us to provide moisture to the ground, air to the plant roots and to increase the fertility of the soil. Mixing fire and air allows us to keep the torches burning."

"You'll see that almost everything we do involves the use of spectrum in some way or another. I used it to get us to Remin. I used it to leave a trace in your bathtub that could be followed by my friends to get back to your house. Remin can't function without it." Houdin paused.

"But Thane must realize that," David said, wrinkling his forehead in confusion.

"Thane understands all too well. He believed that we needed to reduce our dependence on spectrum, and he stole the Imaginator to teach us a lesson. But he became intoxicated by the power and now he cares only about himself." Houdin stopped, for they had arrived at the pier.

David found himself looking at a dilapidated old wooden dock that jutted out into the lake. The pilings were covered with green algae that hung in long streamers and undulated in the water. Several pieces of old rope were tied at various places along the pier and hung down into the water. The silence was broken only by the sound of the gentle lapping of the water.

Houdin asked David to turn around slowly so that he could survey the situation. The assessment was not good. There appeared to be no way to get across the lake. "I don't suppose you could swim across?" Houdin asked.

David looked across the lake and said, "I'm getting much better at swimming, but I can't go that far without something that floats to help me." He glanced around and looked at the dead cornstalks behind him. "I have an idea."

David quickly gathered a large stack of stalks. He snapped off the stalks and continued to shuttle between the field and the beach until he had a large pile. He then went to the pier and got several pieces of rope to tie the stalks together. When he pulled on the last piece of rope, a box came up. Inside the box he could hear a scuttling sound.

He found a small door on the top of the box with a metal latch. He opened the latch and cautiously peered inside. A crab-like animal peered up at him from two big eyes mounted on long stalks. David tipped the box over and began to shake it gently to release the trapped animal. He almost dropped the box when he heard a voice burst out, "Hey, be a little careful there. I may have a hard shell but I've still got feelings." The voice was sarcastic and agitated. A crab tumbled onto the pier. David set aside the box and peered at his new friend (for everybody and everything was always a new friend to him).

The little crab scuttled to the edge of the pier for a quick escape and then paused to look at David. "Well . . . what are you staring at? I guess I should be grateful. I've been trapped in that box for days. It hasn't been easy getting food so I'm a little bit cranky. My name is Cruster."

David smiled, "I'm David and I'm trying to get across the lake to the city. Can you help me?"

Cruster's eyestalks swiveled around like periscopes. "I can't help you directly but I can give you some advice." Cruster's voice then began a singsong cadence as he recited, "The circle spins. No passage here. A one-way downward trip. When caught, left beats right when deciding which way to steer; the way is open with just a sip." Cruster finished and stepped off the pier, vanishing with a splash.

David jumped up and cried out "What does that mean?" There was no answer—just the spreading ripples that marked the departure of the little crab. David sighed, freed the rope from the trap and trudged back to the pile of stalks. After several false starts, he got the pile of stalks bundled together using the ropes.

"Houdin, do you know what Cruster meant by his riddle?"

Houdin had been silent for quite a while and David wondered what the wizard was thinking. Houdin did not answer right away but David could feel the now familiar tickling in his right ear so he knew that Houdin was still there. When at last the wizard spoke, he sounded tired and discouraged. "Parts of the riddle are clear. The lake is protected by whirlpools that respond to movement in the water, so the circles that spin must refer to the whirlpools. The rest of it is unclear. If we get caught in a whirlpool we'll be pulled down and drowned. I have some blue spectrum left which should help us in our passage across the lake. I may be able to fool the lake so that our movements won't trigger the whirlpools. If we do get caught, we'll have to improvise." He did not sound encouraging.

David dreaded the journey across the lake after listening to Houdin. But he wanted to help and he wanted to see the city, so he rolled the bundle of stalks to the water's edge and waded into the lake. The water was tolerable in temperature and soon David was paddling toward the city with the makeshift raft held in front of him. Houdin warned him not to make big splashes and movements. The wizard began to mumble quietly and

David guessed that he was trying to hide them from the lake whirlpools. They made quick progress, and Houdin's efforts seemed to be paying off. The lake remained quiet and undisturbed. They were now close enough to the city to see the high walls and David could see shapes moving along the top of the walls. Probably guards, he thought.

Houdin interrupted his thoughts, "Paddle a little faster, I'm almost out of blue spectrum." The urgency in the wizard's voice was plain. David began to kick harder but he was getting tired. He was looking for someplace to enter the city and he could see an archway similar to the one on the other side of the lake so he aimed for that.

Suddenly the water on his right began to swirl. The swirling quickly became a whirlpool, which began to move toward them. David paddled faster but realized that the bundle slowed him down, so he pushed it away and began to move away from the oncoming funnel. Keeping his right ear above the water required a lot of concentration. David was getting tired both mentally and physically. The whirlpool turned faster and David began to feel the pull of the water on his feet. The next thing he knew he was swept onto the edge of the whirlpool and began to spiral around the edge in a clockwise fashion. The pull on his legs became greater. "Houdin, do something!" David began to panic but Houdin remained silent.

David remembered the words of Cruster's riddle as it became harder and harder to keep his head up. He was beginning to be pulled into the center of the whirlpool. The water was now towering over his head as it spun around him. The circle spins. Well, David thought, that's certainly right. A one-way downward trip. Glancing downward, he could see that the whirlpool went all the way to the bottom of the lake. The sand of the lake swirled madly at the end of the funnel. Left beats right. What did that mean?

Then David had an idea. He was spending all his energy trying to go up. The whirlpool was pulling him to the right; he should be trying go left. He turned and began to swim against the clockwise spiral. He arms felt like lead weights; his legs were like jelly; but if they didn't get out of this soon . . . well he didn't even want to think about it. It seemed like forever, but David noticed that he wasn't being pulled down anymore. Finally, the power of the whirlpool broke. It stopped spinning.

"Houdin, we did it," he yelled, spitting out water. Then the water dropped out from under David. The whirlpool stopped its circling motion and David fell straight down.

He found himself standing on the bottom of the lake in the center of the stationary whirlpool. It was like standing in a funnel that went all the way to the bottom of the lake. He could see the waters of the whirlpool swirling behind an invisible wall, which protected David, who was now standing and looking upward to the sky. In the water beyond the wall he could see different types of fish being swept along in the eddies of the whirlpool.

As David watched these fish, he saw two creatures staring at him and trying to keep their place in the current. They looked like green sea-serpent sock puppets. They had flat elongated noses and bodies that appeared to be all tail. Four tiny legs stuck out near the end of each long body and tiny winglets fluttered along with the thrashing tail as the creatures continued to observe him from behind the wall of water. One eye was set on each side of their heads, but right now these eyes were swiveled forward to stare at him through the rushing water. As David watched them, they suddenly lost the battle to maintain their position in the whirlpool stream and went spinning off in the current.

He wondered what to do next when he noticed that he was standing on a large iron door. In the center of the door was a wheel, but when he tried to turn the wheel he found that it was locked. In the center of the wheel was a funnel, shaped to look like a miniature whirlpool made of metal with a round-hinged cover. David examined the wheel and turned his head so Houdin could also give his opinion, but the wizard was at a loss to solve the mystery as he had never been captured by a whirlpool and released at the bottom of the lake. David finally reached over and flipped up the hinged cover revealing an empty hole. Now what, he thought.

Houdin suddenly interrupted, "The riddle said something about a sip…do you think lake water will help?"

David quickly went over to the side of the whirlpool and tried to touch the water. It felt like gelatin as he touched the wall, and when he pushed a little harder his hand pushed through the wall until he could feel the swirling water beyond. The wall collapsed around his wrist. David pushed his other hand through the wall and cupped his hands in the swirling stream. He slowly brought his cupped hands back out of the wall.

The spell holding the whirlpool back appeared to break as he pulled his hands free because the sand under his feet began to fill with water. The whirlpool was collapsing! David hurried over and dumped the water into the hole and tried the wheel again. The wheel did not turn. The water now was at his ankles. Soon, he wouldn't be able to open the door even if he could turn the wheel.

And then it came to him. He reached down into the rapidly rising water and got another handful, which he quickly poured into his mouth. He then went to the wheel and allowed the water to dribble out of his mouth into the hole at the top of the small metal whirlpool. The door on the top of the little metal whirlpool snapped shut and the tiny whirlpool began to spin. When it stopped, David spun the wheel and the door opened. The rising water began to cascade into the hole revealed by the open door.

David could see light in the hole and a ladder. Quickly he swung down into the hole and started down the ladder with the water pouring down on him. As he reached the bottom of the ladder, the door above him swung shut with a resounding clang. The clang of the closing door faded away, and the fountain of water tapered into a steady drip with a sound like rain.

David's eyes adjusted to the changing light and he saw that he was on the side of a wide tunnel with a road running down the middle. The tunnel was lit by torchlight and he could see that these torches resembled the ones at the entrance to the archway. Every other torch was burning and now he could hear the familiar sound of spectrum being added to the glowing flames.

Houdin's voice startled him with a loud whoop of celebration. "You did it! We're in the entrance tunnel to Remin City. Turn to your left and head down the road."

David grinned and started off down the tunnel. They had been almost to the city when crossing the lake so it didn't take very long to traverse the tunnel and reach the end. The tunnel widened and David could see a large town circle right in front of him.

In the center of the circle was a dome-like structure and moving around the dome was a land-based creature that looked exactly like a five-foot jellyfish. David's eyes were wide in amazement as he tried to take all the sights in. He could see a variety of houses arrayed around the circle, which was intersected by several streets. Each house had a tall narrow door made of wood. Intricate and unique door carvings distinguished each home from its neighbors.

David suddenly heard a noise behind him in the tunnel and shrank back in the shadows, making himself as small as possible. Moments later a horse pulling a cart passed by him. The back of the cart was piled high with fish, and walking behind the cart with a rod and a net was a tired fisherman. Once the cart had passed, David stepped out of the tunnel. Houdin told him to turn to the right and enter the first street he came to.

David wasn't sure where they were going but he followed the directions. At the first street he turned right and began to move away from the circle. He was full of questions about what he was seeing but Houdin wasn't interested in explaining anything right now. After a short walk, Houdin suddenly ordered David to stop. The house they were standing in front of had the same kind of door that he had seen on the circle. The carving on the door looked like a teardrop surrounded by small stars and bordered by vines.

"Who lives here?"

Houdin laughed, "I do."

4 ✳ WALLS AND WANDS

"We need to get inside quickly," sighed Houdin. "We need to get in touch with Kira. She can help us much more than I can in my current state."

David looked at the door again. "How do I get in?"

"Easy, just do what I tell you," said Houdin. "First, push the second star from the right and then the seventh star from the right."

David saw that all the carved stars on the door were actually buttons. He quickly reached out and pushed the stars that Houdin had mentioned. As soon as the seventh star popped back out the teardrop on the door swiveled around revealing a face. David was so startled he took a step back, for the face staring at him looked very much like Thane that he had seen in his dream. The only difference was that this face looked very peaceful.

The eyes stared at him and then David heard a very familiar voice, "Welcome. Password please," said the voice of Houdin, but it wasn't coming from his ear; it was coming from the face on the door.

So that's what Houdin looks like, thought David. He smiled. The door smiled back.

"The password is puffer fish," whispered the Houdin in his ear.

David immediately said, "Puffer fish," to the door.

The face in the door frowned. "That password is correct but only Houdin knows that password and he has not been here for many years. How did you come by that answer?"

David had a feeling of déjà vu as he repeated what he had told the Remin portal door. "Houdin has been transformed into a caterpillar by a curse and is currently sitting in my ear." Again it sounded quite silly.

Unlike the uncooperative portal, Houdin's door greeted them in an amiable voice. "Oh, well, that's a reasonable explanation," it said. "Tell the wizard, I said hi." And with that the face swiveled around again to become a teardrop shape and the door swung open on creaky hinges.

David stepped inside and as he cleared the threshold, the door swung shut again. David turned to look and found the face now looking at him from the inside of the door.

Houdin's voice suddenly erupted in his ear, "If I ever get back to my normal self, that door is going to get a good talking to. How dare it let just anyone in that happens to give the correct password. I can't believe it. What kind of security is that? I might as well just take the door off the hinges . . ."

David laughed, "We're inside. I thought that's what we were trying to do."

Houdin's tirade spluttered to a halt. "But—but—yes, yes, you're right." Houdin got himself calmed down and then said, "I've been thinking about what we should do first and it occurs to me that the tasks before us will require someone who can be a true wizard, and alas, in my present state, I cannot fulfill that role. I think you have some potential. If you would accept, I am willing to help you. David, what do you say?"

"Do you mean you'll help me to become a real wizard?" exclaimed David, his voice rising.

"It's not that easy. Not everyone can be a wizard. Only if you understand how nature is all connected can you use the power of spectrum to influence the things around you in what can only be described as magic. You must respect all living things and

you must be focused on everything that your senses can detect—
the wind on your cheek, the ground beneath your feet, the sun
on your face. If you have the ability, it will soon become obvious.
I can show you how to be a wizard, but only you have the power
to translate those teachings into magic." Houdin hoped that
David would not be discouraged. He didn't need to worry.

Being able to use real magic was one of David's greatest wishes and here was Houdin offering to grant that wish.
Without any more hesitation, David practically screamed, "Of
course. Teach me everything. I'll do my best. Wait until Mom
and Dad see me as a real wizard."

But David's enthusiasm was cut short when Houdin
interrupted, "I'm sorry, but you won't be able to use magic in
your world. Remin is the key to using the power of spectrum.
Because I come from Remin I was able to tap into its power
while in your world. While you are in Remin, you can use that
power as well but once you return to your world the ability to
use spectrum will be lost. My power is very weak when I am in
your world and with no wand, and my size as an added disad-
vantage, I was lucky to even get us here. No, I'm sorry David
but you can only be a wizard while you are in Remin."

David thought about this and then his enthusiasm came
flooding back. "That's OK," he said enthusiastically. "It's better
than never being a wizard. What's next?"

"I think my study is our first stop. Go to the wall in
front of you."

David paused to look around. He was standing in an
eight-sided room that appeared to contain only one door. The
front door was behind him. There was nothing else in the room.
A dusty, gold-colored throw rug was in the center of the room,
and the walls held several paintings in ornately carved wooden
frames. There was nothing special about the paintings from what
David could see. One was a portrait of Houdin (assuming that the
face in the front door was an accurate representation of the cursed
wizard). The other paintings showed various rural scenes that you
would see in any house: a picnic under a sparkling colorful sky, a

sailboat with one of the jellyfish people that David had seen in the square, and a sunset surrounded by a rainbow.

Houdin, who was focused only on the tasks ahead, could not appreciate all the wonderful things that David was trying to absorb. "Well what are you waiting for?"

David jerked out of his trance and walked over to the wall opposite the front door. As he approached the wall, it suddenly became a revolving door, which David quickly stepped through. He turned to look as he stepped into the next room and found another plain wall. The door was gone. He found himself in a cozy little room containing a desk with a comfortable chair and a fireplace. Behind the desk were several shelves. One shelf held very old books. David glanced at the titles of the books and hoped he would get a chance to read While You Were Sleeping: A History of Dreamweaving, How to Weave Authentic Monsters, or maybe Words and Wands: Spellcasting, and The Power of Words: The Greatest Spells Ever. He hoped he didn't need Wizarding for Dummies. The next shelf held a jewelry box and a small crystal ball mounted on a round wooden platform. The last shelf held a much larger glass ball but inside this one pink lightning bolts were shooting around inside.

As David looked around, a fire suddenly ignited in the fireplace. The room, which was quite cold when David entered, soon began to warm up.

"Can I get anything for you?"

Startled, David turned around to find that the face from the front door was now situated on the wall where David had entered the room. As amazing as this was, David was sure he would see many extraordinary things in this magical place. Next to the face was a crystal chess board on a rolling table. "It looks like Houdin must play chess with the face," thought David. He drew a funny picture in his head of Houdin slumped over the chess board while the face was thinking of its next move. With that happy thought, David moved around the desk and settled himself into the chair.

"Fine, ignore me!" the face huffed.

David's face flushed. "I'm sorry, all of this is so new to me, I've forgotten my manners. I don't need anything right now. Thank you for being there for me."

The face brightened considerably, "It's been a long time since I've had anyone to talk to. Since Houdin left, I've had only a couple of mice for company. You might want to ask the old wizard to get rid of them when he gets the chance."

David decided to make the face in the wall feel a little special and spent the next couple of minutes recounting his adventure so far. Houdin tapped his many legs, tickling David's ear until the story ended. Finally, the face relaxed into a serene expression, but the eyes continued to move back and forth, observing the entire room.

With one final tap of his legs, Houdin said, "Now let's get on with it. Open the right-hand side top drawer."

"I'm sorry," said David, then he swung around in the chair and pulled open the drawer. He looked inside and gasped. The drawer was filled with magic wands. David had used all sorts of sticks and toys as pretend wands, but here was the real thing. There were many different kinds of wands made of wood, glass, and stone. All the wood and stone ones were intricately carved with strange symbols and runes. Some of them had pictographs on them that David recognized as Egyptian hieroglyphics. David admired all the wands but the glass wands were the ones that captured his attention. The intricate designs David saw on the wood and stone wands paled in comparison to the patterns on the glass wands. The design of the wands allowed them to capture the light in the room and use it to create subtly shifting shafts of color.

"Do any of these wands stand out in your eyes?" queried Houdin, who was leaning out of David's ear trying to look down into the drawer himself.

"How do I choose the right one?" asked David, but Houdin's reply didn't help.

"I have collected many wands over the years. Some were gifts and others I found in my wanderings. I don't understand everything about each one. They all have their own story and their own unique way of harnessing and concentrating power. Choosing a wand is a personal choice. The wand and the user must work together to give a wizard control over magic. There is no wrong choice."

David tried to look at each wand. He picked up several of the wooden ones but he found that the patterns on them were influencing his choices. The plain wands didn't interest him and that was disturbing because he knew that picking a wand based only on appearance would be the worst way to make his choice. A plain wand would be ignored and it might be the better wand. For that reason, and the fact that his eyes were continually being drawn back to the glass wands, he decided that a glass wand was his destiny. He removed all the glass wands in the drawer and spread them out on the desk.

"Ah, the most difficult wands to decipher are the ones you are now examining," mused Houdin. "Because the light is constantly changing the patterns within the wand, the true power of the wand is hidden."

Once all the wands were spread out in the light, David noticed that each wand consisted of two parts, a rod surmounted by a container. Each container was a different shape and some of the containers had flecks of spectrum inside. David found that his eyes kept returning to one particular wand. This wand had a flask-like container that looked like the spectrum flasks that were keeping the torches lit in the Remin entrance tunnel. David picked up the wand and examined it in the light. The light inside the wand had a smoky quality and as David turned the wand the smoke swirled upward toward the flask. The bottom bulb of the flask tapered upward to a narrow neck that curved with a delicate flare around the tiny hole in the top. Several colored ribbons rippled from the point where the flask joined the long glass shaft. As David gripped the wand and moved it back and forth, the glass absorbed more and more light and brightened. He tightened his grip and the wand got warmer. It felt so right that he immediately knew this was the one. "Can I use this one?"

Houdin looked at the wand. "Interesting that you would choose that one. It was given to me by a friend who made it from a piece of melted glass he found in a crater near his house."

David immediately put it down. "It was a gift, I can't take it." He was disappointed.

Houdin wouldn't take no for an answer. "I have plenty of wands as you can see. A wand wants to be used. Please accept it as a gift from me."

David picked up the wand again. "Thank you, Houdin. I will do the best I can to learn how to use this wand to help you." He carefully replaced all the other wands into the drawer of the desk and closed the drawer. He held the wand up and the face on the wall suddenly came to life again and whistled. David laughed and carefully placed the wand in his jacket pocket.

"Well I think the next thing to do is to try out that new wand of yours and see if we can find out what's been going on since I've been away," said Houdin.

The wizard's voice sounded muffled as if the voice was being blocked from going directly into David's ear. "Houdin, can I see you for a minute?" said David as he held his finger up to his ear. He felt the tickling on his finger, which meant the caterpillar wizard was now on his finger. He brought his hand down in front of his eyes prepared to squint at the diminutive magician and was surprised to see that the caterpillar was now as fat as a pencil and as long as his little finger. David was so startled he almost dropped the caterpillar. "You can't be this big already!" he exclaimed. "You just hatched out this morning. How can you be this big?"

Houdin sighed so loudly that David could hear the little hiss and see the little body sag on his finger. Houdin had to shout again because he was no longer speaking directly into David's ear. "I told you. Time moves much faster here. I follow a normal cycle in your world but once we came here to Remin, things have speeded up. Staying in your ear is becoming quite cramped and it's only going to get worse." Houdin paused to think about the problem. "OK, change of plans. Let's first go to the lab and get some spectrum, then see if we can make some better arrangements for traveling together."

David looked at the sleeping face on the wall. "How do we get to the lab? There's only one door and it goes to the front hall?" He held his finger up near his ear to hear the reply, "Just think about the lab and go through the door."

Carefully holding his finger in front of him, David approached the face. It woke up and winked at David. David touched the wall and it transformed into a door again and swung open. He stepped through the door, thinking about what he envisioned a wizard's lab would look like, and was amazed to find that, instead of standing in the front hallway of the house, he was now in a room that didn't quite look like his idea of a lab, but that was clearly meant to serve that purpose. He spun around to look back into the study and instead found a blank wall again. The face was gone!

He turned back around to survey the lab. He found himself at the end of a long room containing many shelves and a long table running down the center of the room. The shelves were filled with books, bottles and jars of various sizes and shapes, as well as odd gadgets and machines which David couldn't even begin to identify. The center table had some scattered papers, quills, and glass containers, a set of scales, an intricate machine with many levers and gears surmounted by a large funnel. David's eyes were drawn to the set of scales. It was shiny and gold-colored with intricate chains holding up a set of silver dishes. Next to the scales were four very large round glass containers, which were filled almost to the brim with spectrum. Each container appeared to hold only one type of spectrum. The brilliant blue of the water crystals, blazing red of fire, the dazzling silver of the air crystals and the emerald glitter of the earth crystals. Scattered around the four containers were smaller vials containing uniquely colored spectrum. David could see gold, purple, pink, and black. The brightness of the magic glitter transformed the drab room into a brilliant series of rainbows from the reflected sunlight shining through a large window at the far end of the room.

"Breathtaking, isn't it?" said a voice behind him in a bored singsong voice. David turned to face the wall again and, though it had been blank a moment ago, he now found the face smiling at him from its usual position where the door to the room would be. "Yes, I can't get over the . . ." but David was suddenly interrupted by a repetitive tapping on his finger. He looked down to see Houdin attempting to get his attention. He held his finger to his ear.

"I need to be able to speak with you. Please pick up the loader directly in front of you on the table." David looked at the table and saw a small device that resembled a gun with four round containers mounted on the barrel. It was miniature version of the large containers on the table. David picked up the loader and saw that each container had a small, calibrated dial underneath it at the joining to the barrel. He stared at the loader as he again moved his finger to his ear. "Now pretend each dial is a clock and set the hand to the mark that represents the '3'."

David turned each dial to the correct mark. He was starting to see where all this was going. He placed Houdin on the table, removed his new wand from his pocket, and placed the tiny end of the barrel over the opening to the flask at the top of the wand. He then bent down close to the edge of the table to hear Houdin again. "Good, now fill the wand's spectrum reservoir by pressing the trigger." David then balanced the two objects, his wand in his left hand and connected to the loader, which he held in his right hand. He eased back on the trigger. There was a slight 'pop,' and the flask filled with spectrum.

David pulled his wand off of the loader and examined the fully loaded spectrum container. All four types of spectrum were mixed together in the wand and David realized that the dials on the loader were used to set how much of each type of spectrum were loaded into the wand. He put the loader on the table, grinned at the newly loaded wand, then bent to hear what his teacher wanted to say.

"Excellent. You catch on fast. I want you to join our minds so that I can speak to you without shouting. The key to any magic is to believe that the actions you take are possible. Imagine that you can talk to me by just thinking what you want me to hear and that I can do the same to you. Once you have this image in your mind, use the wand to draw an imaginary line between your head and mine and say the words, 'Vulcanius mindmeldium.' Can you do that?"

David nodded. "Wouldn't it be better to wait for Kira? I do want to be a wizard but it might be better if you work with someone older."

It was tough for David to volunteer to step aside but he wanted to do what was best. Houdin quickly made him feel better, "No, I've said it before…magic is dependent on imagination. The people of Remin for the most part lack the imagination to be great wizards. Those of us that show a particular aptitude for this are immediately identified and trained. Kira doesn't have the ability. The people of the your world are much better suited for this, and you seem to have the kind of imaginative, questing mind that is required. Let's try."

David repeated the instructions and then practiced the words and actions until Houdin bobbed up and down with approval. Once he was ready, he took a deep breath and began to imagine the connection between Houdin and himself. He began to trace the line between the two of them and when he felt that the image in his mind was real, he gripped his wand tightly and spoke the words, "Vulcanius mindmeldium." Nothing happened.

"You have to be focused on the spell and you have to imagine that it is possible to establish this connection," lectured Houdin.

"This is hard," grumbled David.

"If being a wizard was easy, there would be wizards everywhere," said Houdin. "Do you know how many wizards there are in Remin? One…and that's me, unless they've found others while I've been away." David could hear how proud Houdin was as he added, "It's the hardest profession in the world. Wands and spectrum only serve as catalysts for the power of a wizard. By themselves, they are useless. Even spectrum is powerless without the imagination and focus of a true wizard's mind."

"What if I can't do this?" asked David. "Won't we need magic against Thane?"

"Well, it should be possible to get to Thane without magic and even to emerge victorious against him, but magic would certainly make it easier," chuckled Houdin. "Coming from your world gives you an advantage. Let's try it again."

David rubbed his head and settled himself. He placed an image in his mind of a telephone call between himself and Houdin. He tried again. His wand flickered. "Did you see that Houdin? I did it!" But the spell didn't work. When he lost his focus the wand dimmed.

"Try using the face on the wall as a model to focus on," Houdin suggested. "It might work better since that's what I really look like." The face immediately began preening—turning to the left and to the right, sticking his chin out, and smiling. David laughed and then grew serious again. This was much harder than he thought. He had always thought that magic would make things easy. Now it appeared that the real magic was inside him.

He refined the image in his mind and pictured Houdin talking on the telephone to him. He performed the spell again, "Vulcanius mindmeldium." Immediately, the wand grew warm and light swirled within the wand. A tiny glitter of spectrum appeared suspended in a straight line between Houdin and David. There was a tiny crackle of power and the line vanished. David felt a tiny shock, like static electricity, in the center of his forehead and suddenly Houdin's voice was there in his head clear and loud as if Houdin were standing there talking to him, "Testing, one, two, three. Testing. Is this thing on?"

David laughed, "This is amazing. It worked. I can hear you loud and clear." Houdin's voice came into his mind again, "OK, I can hear you fine when you speak but can you do it in your mind without speaking out loud." David was embarrassed. Of course, that was the whole reason for this spell. To be able to speak with Houdin without speaking out loud. He tried to speak to Houdin without moving his lips and after several false starts finally figured out that he had to focus on the image of Houdin and then just think of what he wanted to say. Soon he was walking around the room keeping up a running conversation with the wizard and enthusing over all the things in the room. He quickly got used to communicating with Houdin through the magic of the mind meld. It came very naturally to him. He believed in the magic and his strong imagination made the bond between them even greater. Even so, the link was lost between them several times whenever David lost his focus. He had to repeat the spell each time to get the link back.

David put Houdin on the table in the lab. Then he followed Houdin's instructions through the mind meld, went into the study and retrieved a large jewelry box from the shelf behind the desk along with a small sculpture of a dragon. He returned to the lab with the box and placed it next to Houdin. He was puzzled about why Houdin had asked for the dragon until the wizard explained that the key to the jewelry box was actually the tail of the dragon. David used the tail in the lock and opened the box.

As he threw back the lid on the box he had to shield his eyes from the bright light that flashed from the many jewels and glittering metal that filled the box. As his vision cleared, he saw a small horse trinket leap out of the box and attempt to escape. "That's an enchanted stallion. If I can ever find the enchanted saddle that goes with him, you could run as fast as a horse while carrying the medallion," huffed Houdin, who had to swing his hindquarters out of the way of the escaping horse in order to avoid being trampled. David grabbed an empty glass container from the table and upended it over the horse.

Houdin climbed up the box and began to burrow into the jewelry. David could hear him muttering away and soon he exclaimed, "Aha, this should be perfect. David, can you remove the top layer of jewelry and retrieve the necklace that I am wrapped around?"

David did as he was asked and pulled out a beautiful silver chain with an amulet threaded on it. Houdin had wrapped himself around the chain. The amulet consisted of a silver cage with a small stone mounted on either side. Both stones were made of some kind of substance that captured the light and made them look like they were alive. As David looked at them, he had the funny sensation that he was looking much deeper into the stones than was possible. One of the stones was a golden yellow while the other was shimmering silver. The central cage was empty but it looked to David like it had once held a much larger stone.

While David looked at the empty cage, Houdin suddenly slithered down the chain and settled himself into the cage. David smiled. Now it was all clear. He could wear the necklace and Houdin could travel in comfort and still see everything. The sun was beginning to set as David admired the glinting amulet in the fading rays of light coming through the window. With everything that was happening, he failed to see that there was a small mouse outside the window taking an unusual interest in the activities in the room.

"What am I looking at, Houdin?" queried David in his normal voice. David suddenly realized how sleepy he felt. He couldn't keep up the focus necessary to converse with Houdin through the melding and so he reverted to speaking out loud. The link between them began to fray. Even though he wasn't trying to maintain the link, the power of his thought was keeping it open but his focus was slipping. To the mouse, observing the room, David appeared to be alone and looking through Houdin's things while talking to himself.

Houdin noticed the switch back to normal speech and the tired quality of the voice and realized with some embarrassment that he was pushing the little boy far beyond his abilities. Despite his need to find Thane again, he knew that David needed sleep and so he postponed his plans. "I'm sorry. I haven't been a very good host. Let's get you settled in a bed and I'll tell you the story of this amulet tomorrow. After that we can find out what's going on and make plans. Let's get you into bed."

David was so tired he didn't even try to argue and with thoughts of a warm, soft bed running through his head, he approached the wall where the door should be. The face slid into view as the door opened and David shuffled into Houdin's bedroom holding the amulet in his hand. He hung the amulet on a hook near the face in the wall so that Houdin could talk to the face while he slept. He slipped his shoes off and climbed under the covers of what seemed to him to be the most comfortable bed in the world. As tired as he was, he couldn't resist asking one more question. "What's so important about the amulet?"

Houdin, who had been conversing with the face in the wall, stopped and sent his reply to David's tired mind. "This amulet was the key to finding out about Thane's treachery." But even as he said it, he realized that David wasn't listening anymore. The link between them vanished as sleep took over for the tired novice wizard. The soft sound of snoring filled the wizard's darkened bedroom. Houdin whispered a suggestion and immediately the room was filled with a soft glow emanating from a wizard face nightlight. Behind the glow, the face was smiling.

Neither Houdin nor David saw the mouse leap down from the window and scamper away.

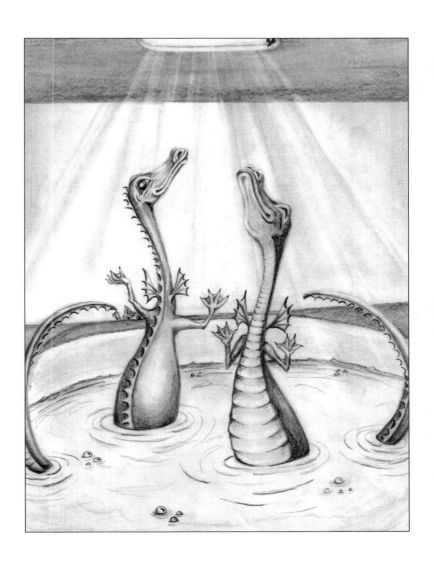

THE MONSTERS
5 * IN THE BATHTUB

For the first time in many nights, David's sleep was not interrupted by dark dreams. When the sun began sending its warmth through the bedroom window and across the heavy comforter on the bed, David opened his eyes. For an instant, his heart sank, for his first thought was that the events of last night had been a fantastic dream, but as he sat up, he saw that he was not in his own bed, there was an animated wizard face on the wall opposite the bed and hanging next to the face was an amulet with a tiny silver cage. He felt refreshed and ready to continue the adventure.

He found that his hand was clenched tightly around his wand. He had slept with his wand and it was painful even to open his fingers. He looked at the amulet hanging next to the glowing wizard face. Then he placed the image of the telephone connection in his mind and performed the melding spell. The first time didn't work but the second time he got it right. He smiled as his thoughts were suddenly interrupted by the cheery voice of a refreshed (although cursed) wizard.

"Good morning," said Houdin. "We need to get started. I'm sorry but after being gone for so long there is no edible food in the house except some dried fruit. We'll have to delay a real breakfast until we get in touch with Kira, but we should be able to make do with the fruit and a rehydration spell."

David couldn't have cared less about breakfast. He threw back the covers and leaped out of bed. As if he had lived here all his life, he thought about the bathroom. He grabbed the amulet as he stepped through the door and went into the bathroom. A few minutes later he stepped through the door again, thinking about the kitchen. On the table was a bowl of what could barely be described as dried fruit: small hard balls, which used to be apples and oranges. Under Houdin's directions, David took out his wand and, waving it over the bowl, used the Hydroswellium spell, which sent a sprinkle of blue spectrum mixed with flecks of silver over the dried fruit. The sprinkles lay there but the fruit did not change.

David realized that keeping the meld going with Houdin while he attempted this new spell was too confusing. He put all his focus on the fruit and tried again. He was rewarded with a warm glowing wand and watched in amazement as the apples and oranges expanded rapidly to their original size and color. In the next instant he was devouring the best tasting five-year-old apple in the world. Cold, crisp and juicy. He hadn't realized how hungry he was until now, so he helped himself to another one and finished breakfast off with an orange.

He performed the melding spell again and this time got it on the first try. He offered some fruit to Houdin but Houdin explained that the curse sustained him. "What good would a repeating curse be if you could break it by starving yourself to death," he mused. "No, the curse is too clever for that. If I eat nothing, I continue to feel nourished, which is a good thing, since I hate the taste of milkweed!" Houdin waited until David ate the last of the orange and then directed him to the study, where a new fire kindled itself to warm the room.

"Before we start, my wooden counterpart wonders if you could refill the torches in the house. The spectrum was exhausted long ago and when the sun goes down the house is completely dark."

"Sure," said David. "I don't like the dark, either."

They went to the lab where Houdin pointed out a device that would do the job. David used the spectrum loader to fill the device with red spectrum and then following Houdin's instructions, wandered from room to room refilling the flasks of the long cold torches. The face followed him and enthused about how nice it was going to be to watch over a house it could see at night. David grinned, finished filling the torches and wandered back into the study.

He continued to be amazed each time he stepped through the door in the wall and found himself in a different room. Each time the door was different. Sometimes it was a wood-paneled door, other times it might be white or yellow, or green. Pictures appeared and disappeared on the wall that held the door. For example, when he entered the study this time and looked at the wall, it held a small picture of a rainbow with the face grinning under the arch. Last night the wall had been bare. It was like being in a house where some mad decorator was constantly going around rearranging things.

Houdin was eager to implement the plan he had been hatching all night. "We need to contact Kira. I discussed this with old wooden head..." David glanced at the face on the wall, which grimaced and stuck out its tongue, "and we came up with a plan. In order to contact Kira you have to know what she looks like. Once you can picture her in your mind, we can perform the contact. It will be like a telephone call using spectrum."

The face swiveled out of view and Houdin explained the process that they would use to make the call. When the face reappeared on the wall it didn't look like the wizard anymore. The beard was gone and while the Remin nose was still there (David couldn't get the image of a bear out of his mind) the features were much softer and more feminine. The long hair on the Houdin image was replaced by a much shorter style swept to one side of the smiling face. David studied the face for a while and then made the call with a flick of his wand.

"Bellmorsium Kira." Silver spectrum swirled out of the wand and formed a glittering swirling circle, which hovered in front of David. I got it the first time, thought David. Maybe this isn't as hard as I thought. David spoke into the circle, "Kira, I am a friend of Houdin's. He has returned to Remin and needs your help."

He paused and waited, silently watching the glittering spectrum. After a few moments, an excited voice came out of the circle, "Houdin, are you there? Where have you been? We have looked everywhere for you. I thought I would never see you again. I have so much to tell you. Thane is destroying Remin . . ." The voice continued a steady stream of one-sided conversation while David waited to speak. His mind began to wander while he waited for Kira to take a breath. Suddenly, the circle of spectrum hovering in front of him stopped and fluttered to the ground. Kira's voice was abruptly cut off in mid-sentence.

"You lost your focus," chastised Houdin.

David quickly worked to reestablish the call to Kira. When he was able to get the spell to work Kira's voice came through in a rush. "Sure, hang up on me!" She sounded amused. David had been afraid she would be mad but she simply picked up the conversation where it had been interrupted as if the spell had never been broken. David soon found himself waiting for a chance to talk again. Now he could see how hard this whole wizard thing was going to be. He now had to concentrate on the conversation, focus on keeping the spell going and keep the melding between Houdin and himself. His head was throbbing with the effort. He could feel trickles of sweat dripping down his neck. Houdin was muttering to himself and finally told David to interrupt.

"Excuse me," said David. The voice stopped abruptly. Houdin whispered instructions and David relayed them. "Houdin cannot speak to you directly. If you could come to Houdin's house, we could discuss the problem directly and because of the current circumstances, it would help if you brought some kind of food." Kira quickly agreed to come.

David imagined that he was hanging up a telephone and suddenly the glittering circle of spectrum collapsed and fluttered to the floor. He shifted his focus to Houdin and felt better immediately. He was becoming used to the melding spell and found it easier to keep it going while he was doing other things. My dad was right, he thought, practice makes perfect.

"While we are waiting for Kira, I will try to explain the history of this amulet," Houdin said. David settled into the chair behind the desk. He placed his wand on the desk and glanced at the jewelry box that had held the amulet. He removed the amulet and placed it on the desk so that he could see Houdin. The caterpillar crawled out of the silver cage and faced David. Even though they were communicating with their minds, it felt better to be facing each other for this storytelling session. Houdin paused as if trying to decide where to begin.

"Thane has always been a bit of an enigma for us. Early in his life, it was determined that his imagination level was very high but when we tried to train him as a wizard, he failed us."

"So just having imagination is not enough?" said David thoughtfully.

"Apparently not. It appears that Thane's imagination is weighted so heavily toward darkness and evil that he can't see past it. His mind is focused on the stuff of nightmares: ghosts, monsters, human fears, despair. You name it and Thane feeds on it. Once this was recognized, Thane was trained as a dreamweaver."

"You mentioned that before," interrupted David. "I'm not sure it's clear to me the difference between a wizard and a dreamweaver. I also don't understand why you would want Thane to do anything if he's as evil as you believe."

"Wizards can use their imagination independently. They can react to situations with actions based solely on their own thoughts. Dreamweavers need someone else's thoughts to play off of. They can enhance imaginative thoughts but they can't generate those thoughts themselves." Houdin swayed his head toward the window. David looked up into a blue sky covered with black streamers. Houdin continued, "Each of those streamers represents an imaginative thought coming from someone's dream state. While many dreams are just enjoyable diversions, there are always darker thoughts and images that need attention as well."

"Why do we need nightmares at all? I don't see why anything that scares me needs to seem real in my dreams," shuddered David.

"Kira can probably explain it better but it is believed that the brain needs many types of stimulation in order to grow and make new connections. The brain needs to be able to deal with all kinds of situations and it learns while you are sleeping. In order to learn how to deal with the negative emotions experienced in life, the brain needs to be confronted with situations that involve those emotions. Would you rather learn about the fear of falling from actually having to fall or let the brain understand it by experiencing it while you are asleep?"

"I can see your point but what does all this have to do with the amulet?" said David. He found the whole story fascinating. He looked between the sky and the amulet. As he looked between the two, the face of the wizard swiveled into view on the blank wall. The face looked quite annoyed.

"You know this mindmeld stuff doesn't help me at all. I can't hear what's going on and I've been lonely for so long," complained the face.

David sympathized, "I'm sorry. I'll try to include you in the conversation but I can't relay everything Houdin says or the whole story will never come out." The face did not look at all satisfied with that answer but quickly lapsed into a sullen silence.

"As I was saying," said a slightly annoyed Houdin, "the ability to practice dreamweaving on darker thoughts is highly prized here in Remin. When Thane's abilities were discovered, he was encouraged to excel in that area and, I hate to admit it, but he was quite good at it. He . . ." Houdin suddenly stopped his story in mid-thought, interrupted by David and the face who were grinning and whispering conspiratorially. David was doing his best to transfer Houdin's story to the face.

"Just slow down a little bit," David pleaded as Houdin began complaining about the interruptions. "Everything I do here is new to me and talking to a face on a wall is fun. Don't be a party pooper." David stuck out his bottom lip and batted his eyes at the little caterpillar. Houdin sighed and agreed to slow down.

"Thane became convinced that our dependence on spectrum was harmful to our society. We had lost the skills to do anything for ourselves, and if anything should happen to the Imaginator we would be lost. He conceived a plan to steal the Imaginator to teach Remin a lesson.

"Thane was idealistic and charismatic, and he began to attract followers. He grew close to two brothers, Aradel and Folin. Thane convinced Folin to help him steal the Imaginator. It is well known that anyone exposed to the power generated within the dome housing the Imaginator is doomed to certain death. Thane convinced Folin that this healing amulet would allow him to enter the dome, and would protect him while he stole the Imaginator. The amulet at the time was real and Folin believed. He entered the dome and stole the Imaginator. The amulet's power could not compete against the power of the Imaginator and the central stone on the amulet was destroyed. Folin died in intense pain, but not before telling us about Thane. That is the beginning of the..." Houdin stopped and watched as a shadow passed by the window. "Ah, here comes Kira now." The face swiveled out of view.

Houdin crawled back into the cage and David put the amulet back on. He picked up his wand and waited. He could hear a commotion beginning beyond the wall and as he watched a door suddenly appeared in the wall and swung open with a loud bang. David was amazed to see that the wooden wizard face had done pretty well in making a likeness of the person that now entered the room. Even though Kira had Thane's nose and mouth, the hair and eyes were totally different. Short red hair framed her face and emphasized a pair of laughing green eyes. She was dressed like a hunter with tan shirt and brown pants and a white bandana wrapped around her forehead. A coil of rope and a large machete-like knife were the only things that David could recognize arrayed around her waist on a wide leather belt. She began removing a backpack as she surveyed the room.

"Where is he?" she said with a large smile. Her eyes looked closely at David and then checked the room again. She glanced at the face and patted its head, "Good to see you again. Are you glad to have your master back?" The face purred like a kitten and then winked and said, "He's all right but I much prefer your company."

Kira laughed and turned to face David again. "Tell Houdin that he's got a mouse problem. There's a dead mouse on his front doorstep. First one I've ever seen in the city."

The face jumped into the conversation. "Good riddance. Now if his partner could be eliminated, I would be quite happy."

Kira frowned. "You've seen mice around here?" The face nodded. "For the last five years, a pair of mice has been hanging around the house."

Now it was David's turn to frown. "What's the big deal about mice? We have all kinds of mice where I come from."

"It's a little different here," said Kira with a concerned look. "I'll have to talk to Houdin about it later. Now where is he? We have been looking for him with no success."

David quickly summarized his adventure so far and Kira listened with rapt attention. She seemed delighted to see Houdin even in his current condition and she seemed eager to give her side of the story, but just as they were settling in around the desk, she suddenly remembered the request for food and went to get her backpack.

David soon found himself eating crackers and buttered bread while Kira placed a small pot of cream-of-crab soup over the fire. While she busied herself with the soup she was quiet. David assumed she was pondering where to begin. After she dished out some of the soup for David (which was quite good), she settled herself behind the desk. David explained what

Houdin had told him so far, and Kira picked up the story where Houdin had left off.

"With the death of poor Folin, we now knew that Thane had taken the Imaginator. At first we couldn't understand what he sought to gain by possessing it, but we learned to our dismay that Thane's abilities as a wizard were much greater than we had ever thought. He was able to reconstruct the Imaginator and use its power for his own purposes. At first he concentrated on making nightmares scarier than the dreamer needed."

"Why would he want to do that?" asked a very puzzled David.

"We're not completely sure but it appears that Thane has discovered a way to use the emotions being generated by the dreams to build up power for himself. He controls the distribution of spectrum over Remin and he is able to enhance the power of spectrum so that his spells are stronger and more deadly. He feeds off of the power."

"Yes, but when this first started, he wouldn't have been as strong. Why couldn't you get it back then? He's just one person, right?" said David.

Kira sighed. "He convinced others like Folin that he could help them be greater than they were. He gained control over several of the animals of Remin, including mice." She glanced across the room to the entrance hall, as if indicating the dead mouse on the front step. "We made the mistake of not recognizing the threat to be as serious as it was and did not send Houdin to get it back right away. Instead we sent a team of trained volunteers to retrieve the Imaginator. They were unsuccessful. None of them returned."

"Were they killed?" David had thought Thane was bad before this but now he was even worse.

"We thought so at first, but later we found out that Thane had used the power of spectrum to enslave them. Most of the volunteers were mano, another intelligent species that lives in Remin. Mano are very sensitive to spectrum, which gives them great aptitude as dreamweavers. Unfortunately, Thane was able to prey on that sensitivity to control them. Now, they help to guard and protect him."

"Houdin, Folin's brother Aradel, and I finally set out to confront Thane. I saw how Thane was able to snare Houdin. We were not aware that the mice nearby were keeping Thane informed of our movements. He knew we were there, and while Houdin was preparing to capture him, Thane directed his curse at a nearby mirror which rebounded onto Houdin, instantly sending him to your world to begin the endless cycle that you see now."

Houdin's voice suddenly came to David. "So that's how he did it. I was looking at him the whole time and he was facing away from me. I never thought to use a mirror to direct a spell. Ingenious. Thane could have been a great wizard. It's too bad we didn't see it and allowed his darker purposes to prevail."

Kira had stopped talking. It was obvious from David's expression that Houdin was talking. David relayed the conversation to Kira.

Kira continued, "Aradel and I barely escaped. Thane vanished, although there are all kinds of rumors about his whereabouts. We didn't realize that Houdin was not here anymore and we searched for many long years, trying to locate and help him. We have tried to take our best dreamweavers and make them into wizards but have failed miserably. The supply of spectrum has been decreasing. We have instituted all kinds of conservation efforts. There are restrictions in place on almost anything that utilizes spectrum. But it is not enough. Things are rapidly reaching a crisis point."

"But what can we do?" David recognized that he was in over his head. How could he hope to even help these people against Thane? It was ridiculous!

"I've been thinking about that ever since you called," said Kira. "Even an insect Houdin is better than no Houdin at all. His knowledge and leadership have been sorely missed. I will admit that I am at a loss as to what to do next. Thane's whereabouts are unknown. If Thane has spies in the city, it's possible he knows that you are here."

David thought about this. "No one saw us enter the city. We got here last evening through the tunnel and came straight here. Thane can't know anything." Houdin agreed with him.

"I know what to do," Houdin chortled. "Thane's not the only one that knows the value of spies. Tell Kira we're going to talk to Fred and Michelle."

"Of course!" enthused Kira. "Those two troublemakers have an eye on everything."

David was confused. "Where are they and how do we get to them?"

"Oh, we don't have to get to them," laughed Houdin. "They will come to us. And we don't have to even leave the house. We only have to go as far as the bathroom."

Puzzled, David walked over to the wall, thinking about the bathroom. The wall swung open and David and Kira walked into the bathroom. David glanced around. The room was empty. A large circular stone tub was in the center of the room, and around it were a sink, a toilet and a long marble counter. Sunlight shone through a large circular skylight warming the room and highlighting the tub. Kira picked up a rubber stopper from the countertop and handed it to David with a large smile. "Go ahead. Fill the tub."

David placed the stopper (which was quite large) over the large opening in the bottom of the tub. He noticed that the stopper had a long slit running down the center and if he squeezed the stopper the slit would open. He turned the taps and water gushed into the tub.

The face swiveled into view, and in a tone of mock terror said, "No, don't let them in!" Kira laughed and David glanced around confusedly. Even Houdin was laughing.

The tub was full. David turned off the water and carefully followed the whispered instructions from Houdin. He swirled the water in the tub with the end of his wand and spoke the words "Bellmorsium aqua." A jet of pure blue spectrum hit the water and arranged itself around the swirl. When David removed the wand the swirling circle of blue remained. He repeated the spell and stared at the tub, which now contained two swirling blue circles. The circles created miniature whirlpools, which appeared to stretch downward and center on the stopper.

He now touched the center of the first circle with his wand and as he did Kira leaned over called out into the swirling circle, "Fred!" His wand grew warm and the blue spectrum within the circle began to sparkle and flash. As he touched the second circle, Kira called out, "Michelle!" and again the wand and the spectrum reacted. David was having trouble again keeping the spells going. As he concentrated on the swirling water the whirlpools began to collapse. He placed his wand back in the water and concentrated on the spell, and the swirling water once again became two clearly defined whirlpools.

They all stood waiting. Houdin was muttering, "What's taking so long. Where can they be?"

Kira nervously asked, "Do you think they are still around? It's been a long time."

Houdin was thoughtful about the delay, "I've been gone a long time. It would be unrealistic to think that they have been waiting all this time for me." David looked between Kira and the amulet on his neck as he relayed Houdin's comments to Kira. He watched the swirling water and then suddenly the slit in the stopper began to bulge outward. The distortion of the water made it hard to see what was happening, but David thought he could see something moving in the water. His mouth fell open as what can only be described as a sea serpent rose out of the middle of one of the swirling circles.

David recognized the creature as one of the ones that had been watching him in the lake. The serpent resembled a sock puppet even more when seen close-up. Shiny green scales covered its body and its eyes were staring at David and Kira with amusement. As the serpent stared at them, it suddenly jerked and looked downward toward the drain. "Quit shoving. I'll be out of the way in a second." The voice was deep and smooth but slightly sarcastic. "She's always so pushy."

As he spoke, he suddenly swished his tail, which came out of the slit in the stopper, and splashed David and Kira. A second serpent bobbed up into the empty swirling circle. This one was a slightly lighter color with a thinner mouth and shorter nose. "Geez, what were you doing? I've seen turtles faster than that! Have I missed the whole thing?" The voice was much softer and higher but equally amused.

Kira stepped forward. "Ladies and Gentlemen, let me present Fred and Michelle, serpents extraordinaire." The two serpents pirouetted in the water and bowed. David laughed and clapped his hands.

Houdin muttered, "Showoffs," but even he sounded amused.

"Where's Houdin?" Fred was now quite serious, and David for the fourth time explained what had happened and held the amulet out for Fred and Michelle to see the cursed wizard. "Well it could have been worse. You could have been cursed into the life of a dung beetle."

David giggled and Houdin said, "Oh ha ha. There's nothing funny about this."

Kira leaned over the tub. "We're going after Thane again. We are hoping that you've learned things in your wanderings and spying that can help us to . . ."

"Spying? Spying? That's such an ugly word," grumped Michelle. "We prefer to think of ourselves as observant and attentive. You know it's considered quite fashionable to pay attention when other people talk." She raised her nose in the air. "Humph." Fred was nodding agreeably.

Kira sighed, "Oh fine, you're not spies. What have you 'observed' that may help us find Thane?" As she said it, Michelle shuddered and dipped her head and Fred swung his tail in a vicious arc.

Fred swished his tail and began musing about the information they had gathered. "Well let's see, the Perelli boys are skipping school and playing down by the lake; we saw Veron throwing trash into the reservoir; the dreamweavers like to make water spouts in their spare time; Warvel is building a raft; we saw David here defeat the lake whirlpools and we have never seen anyone do that. We got very dizzy watching that one." Fred grinned and both he and Michelle pirouetted around faster and faster. They both laughed when they stopped spinning, swayed back and forth, and rolled their eyes in unison like two clockwork dolls.

"Enough already!" exclaimed Kira. "What about Thane? We can get local gossip from anyone." Even though David was enjoying the two serpents, he was eager to get started as well.

The serpents sobered up, and after a quick glance at each other, Fred said, "We haven't seen Thane but we have some clues that may help. We have asked every creature we knew to keep looking and report anything peculiar and we can report several unusual things that may warrant attention." He paused and looked at Michelle, who nodded with obvious reluctance.

"The waters of Istep Lake have been getting warmer, according to several frogs we talked to who claimed to come from that area; we have observed the streams of dream thoughts in the sky and have seen groups of them diverted from their ordinary paths and headed toward Istep; birds have reported seeing lights in the ruins on the isle of Salvar, in the center of Lake Istep. We believe that Thane is hiding in the east near Lake Istep."

Kira was looking thoughtful. "We need to look at some maps."

Houdin, who had been silent for quite a while, suddenly asked David to break the mindmeld and transfer the amulet to Kira. "I need to discuss some things with her and it would be quicker and easier to do it this way."

David removed the amulet and handed it to Kira. She held the amulet up with the tiny silver cage near her ear and smiled as she heard Houdin shouting as loud as he could. She exited the bathroom, laughing and conversing with Houdin, leaving David and the serpents. None of them noticed the shadow of the mouse that had been peering at them through the skylight and now scampered away.

"David, you have to tell us how you beat the whirlpools. That was a very neat trick." Michelle stared avidly up at David as he explained about Cruster, the riddle and how he had figured it all out just in time. He could hear laughter and murmuring coming from the next room and he wanted to know what was going on, but talking to Fred and Michelle was so enjoyable he figured he could catch up as soon as the serpents left.

Finally, the serpents said goodbye. "As they say in your world, see you later alligator," said Fred.

"After while, crocodile," returned David automatically. "Wait, how do you know what we say in my world?" Fred just winked, then he and Michelle tail-walked around the tub and pretended to be sucked down through the tub stopper. David clapped as the two serpents vanished down the drain and reached into the tub to remove the stopper.

He suddenly jerked his hand away as the water around the stopper began to bubble. He assumed that Fred and Michelle were coming back so he stepped back and watched the roiling water, but the serpents didn't reappear. Instead the water began to steam and bulge. The ghost of a man began to rise out of the water. David could see right through him. He appeared to be made of water and his head was bowed down. Slowly, the head lifted and David's heart began to thump louder and faster as he recognized Thane grinning maniacally in the steaming water.

"You are wasting your time little one," cackled Thane. "Go back where you came from. I was already too powerful for Houdin when he was in his prime, and you think that you can make a difference here? Soon, all of Remin will be crushed and I will rule over everything. Every dream will bend to my will. You are wasting your time."

David was too shocked to run. Thane raised his arms as if to embrace David and began to laugh. The laugh continued as Thane's entire watery body collapsed with a splash and vanished.

"Houdin! Kira!"

The face swiveled into view with a concerned expression. David's panicked cry brought Kira running through the wall, with the swinging amulet clutched tightly in her hand.

"What's wrong?"

"I saw him. He warned me."

"Who?"

"Thane!"

"You saw Thane? Here? Impossible!"

"I tell you, he was here. He came out of the drain. Well, not Thane exactly, but a copy made out of water." David pointed to the tub. The water wasn't moving but steam was still rising.

The face on the wall looked horrified and began wailing, "Intruder alert! Intruder alert! We're doomed!"

"If Thane is able to do that, he's more dangerous than even I imagined," said Houdin. "We've got to get going."

"Where are we going?" David was confused and scared. Thane's appearance had completely unnerved him.

"Why Lake Istep, of course," said Kira. "We'll pack some supplies and pick up Aradel on the way out."

"Aradel? Folin's brother? Where is he?" asked David.

Kira laughed. "He's where he always is. Guarding the power dome in the central plaza."

6 ✳ BROTHER BETRAYED

The next few minutes were a blur of activity. Kira handed David the amulet and disappeared through the door into the lab. As soon as the door closed David stepped through it and entered the study, where several maps were visible on the corner of the desk. The air was still filled with the wailing of the face, which swiveled in the study and then the lab bemoaning the horrors that were coming.

Houdin directed David behind the desk to an ornately carved wooden box. When David opened the box, he found a glass spool. It had the same smoky quality as his wand and he found that the spool fitted neatly over the tiny flask on the wand. The opening of the flask now was in the center of the spool. "What does it do?" He recognized that his wand now resembled the wand that Thane was holding in his dream except his was glass and Thane's appeared to be made of wood.

Houdin sounded thoughtful. "I don't know if you'll have any use for it at all. The dreamweavers all use the spool and if you continue to show promise as a wizard, you may find that you have the ability to use the spool to manipulate dream streams." He listened for a moment to the sounds coming from the lab and then continued, "Besides, this spool goes with the wand you chose. Never break up a set."

They could hear Kira calling them and as David turned to leave the study, he suddenly had an idea. "Houdin, is there room for some books? I would like to borrow some of your books to read. They might help me to become a better wizard." Houdin agreed at once so David took Words and Wands: Spellcasting, and The Power of Words: The Greatest Spells Ever from the shelf. He fanned through them and was happy to see that they weren't in some kind of secret language and he could easily read them.

They moved into the lab where Kira was busy filling four leather sacks with large scoops of spectrum. Once the sacks were filled, she affixed them to a short piece of rope and wrapped it around David's waist. She hung a spectrum loader from the rope belt and then stood back and surveyed him. She gave him a small backpack just big enough to carry the books from the study and declared, "It will do. I don't want to give you too much to carry and if Houdin is right and you have the ability to be a true wizard, then all you need is plenty of spectrum, a loader and a wand. Aradel and I can carry the rest of the supplies. Her hands dropped to her own belt and fingered the coil of rope hanging there. She went back to the study and retrieved her backpack and the maps, returning quickly and stuffing the folded maps into her backpack and together they moved into the barren kitchen. She scooped up the rehydrated fruit and rummaged around for various utensils that she thought they might be able to use. She handed David a short knife in a scabbard that she found hanging from a cabinet handle. David hung the scabbard on his rope belt and held tightly to his wand while he watched Kira looking through the pantry. He could hear her muttering to herself, "There's nothing here we can use. It's all gone bad. Just like Houdin to have only perishables and then disappear for years."

The face had finally stopped wailing and was waiting morosely on the wall, watching the preparations for the journey. "You're leaving me again," it sobbed, "just when we were getting to know each other. It's not fair."

David relayed some instructions from Houdin, which made the face feel needed again, and then while Kira finished stuffing things in her backpack, David leaned over and whispered to the face. He soon had the face laughing and smiling as Kira straightened up and declared, "We're ready. Unless Houdin can think of anything else in this dusty old house."

Houdin pondered the question for a moment but he couldn't think of anything so they moved into the front hallway. The face swiveled into view on the front door, which swung open on rusty hinges to show David a warm sunny morning in Remin. With a quick goodbye, Kira and David moved into the street in front of Houdin's house. The last traces of morning fog were still visible hugging the ground. Kira pointed out the dead mouse lying just outside the door to Houdin's house. "We may be watched," she said quietly, her voice tight with concern.

David turned and, as the teardrop shape on the front door melted into the wooden face, he waved. A small wooden tear formed on the cheek. Then the face gave a slow sad wink and vanished, leaving the usual teardrop shape on the door again.

They retraced David's path from the night before and entered the central part of the city that David had observed from the shadow of the entrance tunnel. David was enjoying the sunlight warming his face as he hurried to keep up with Kira's long strides. When she saw him falling behind, she looked a little chagrined and slowed down. "I'm sorry. I'm rushing. It's been so long and a little longer won't make much of a difference, but I don't want Thane to win." David tried to move a little faster. They passed a fountain and David paused to admire the rainbow visible in the mist from the fountain mingled with fog. The sound of the gently splashing water was the only thing that broke the silence of this early morning in Remin.

The domed building that David had seen last night now loomed in front of them. Houdin confirmed David's thinking by whispering, in a voice filled with emotion, "The Imaginator!" He then corrected himself with some chagrin, "Well, the structure where the Imaginator used to be until Thane took it."

They arrived in front of the dome. The surface of the dome was metallic, gleaming in the sunlight and reflecting a rainbow of colors through the rapidly dissipating fog. The square appeared to be deserted in this early part of the morning, although David could see several people moving on some of the side streets. Kira started to go around the dome, then suddenly stopped as a sudden quick shuffling sound began and grew louder indicating that something was coming from behind the dome.

"Stand back. Behind the yellow line! This area is off-limits." The voice sounded hollow as if the speaker was talking in a tunnel and David stared in amazement at the thing that came around the corner.

Kira smiled broadly and exclaimed, "Aradel, don't be rude. We have guests." But even as she said it, she took two steps back behind a yellow line that David could see was painted on the ground and appeared to encircle the dome. Aradel was a little taller than David but much wider. His skin had a translucent jelly-like quality that reinforced David's initial impression that he was looking at a large jellyfish. He didn't have legs but instead appeared to glide along the ground on a layer of mucus, which followed behind and then vanished as he moved. There were no arms, just globs that stuck out where arms should have been and grew longer and shorter as Aradel approached.

David had to laugh. Here's a man who can't hide anything, he thought, he's just like a glass frog. David could see all of Aradel's internal organs through the skin—his heart, stomach, lungs, and brain. He had a line of eyes that went all the way around his body. Aradel was carrying a variety of weapons, which were all visible on his body. David could see a sword stuck right through his middle. The handle jutted from his side but David could see the whole blade through the skin. Aradel also carried a knife and a baton.

He shuffled up to Kira. "Hello Kira, good to see you," he said, in a tone that didn't seem like he was happy to see her. "Who's your friend?" A glob of mucus formed and waved in David's general direction.

Kira ignored the question, "Aradel, Houdin's back! We're going after Thane again."

David could see all of Aradel's eyes as they rapidly scanned the area. "He's not here! Where is he? Where has he been?"

Kira pointed at the amulet and now answered Aradel's original question. "This is David. He found Houdin in his world, the dream world, and brought him back here. Houdin is under a reincarnation curse but is able to communicate with David. He's using David as a proxy wizard and I must say that David appears to have a lot of aptitude for it. He's already performed several spells and his imagination makes him a very quick study." David's face turned red and he looked down at the ground.

Aradel stared with all his eyes at David. Kira brought Aradel up to speed with current events. She finished the story and asked, "Aradel, will you join us in traveling to the ruins of Salvar and confronting Thane?"

Aradel shuffled backward in horror. "I'm guarding the power dome. I can't desert my post."

Houdin, who had been silent up to this point now intruded on David's thoughts, "What's he guarding? The dome is empty! He's not needed here."

David relayed Houdin's words to Aradel who seemed even more horrified. "The dome could be vandalized. If and when we recover the Imaginator from Thane, the dome will be needed. Without the dome, we won't be able to restore the power to the Imaginator. It's important. Houdin can't malign my work. I have failed Remin by trusting Thane, but now my mind is clear and I won't fail again!" He was almost shouting.

David answered without waiting for Houdin's reply. "No one else wants to harm the Imaginator. Everyone else depends on it. Your world depends on it. Only Thane doesn't see its importance."

"That's not entirely true," Kira corrected. "Thane understands all too well the importance of the Imaginator to Remin and to your world. Let's look inside. I'll tell you about the Imaginator and we'll try to convince Aradel to accompany us."

Aradel grunted and muttered, "Good luck. I'm not coming with you." He shuffled around to the other side of the dome. David and Kira followed. On the other side of the dome was a door with a small porthole in it. David reached for the handle, but Aradel now showed the first signs of amusement, "It's not that simple. The door is locked from the inside."

David was confused. He looked at the door and could now see that there was no lock on the outside. He turned and watched as Aradel put down his sword, baton and knife. He shuffled up to the door and began to melt toward the ground, flattening out and oozing under the door. In seconds Aradel had disappeared. David looked through the porthole and saw Aradel reappear on the other side of the door. A soft click and the door to the dome swung outward and Aradel waved a jelly arm to welcome them into the dome. Houdin breathed, "Amazing. I would never have thought of that. Locking the door from the inside so that only a mano can enter. It's brilliant."

As Kira stepped inside, her face brightened. "A lot has changed since you left, Houdin. The only bright side to this whole affair is that we have learned more about the Imaginator since its theft, then we ever learned while it was here." She gazed around the dome in admiration. "But I guess I better start at the beginning. She gestured around and said, "This is the power dome that housed the Imaginator."

David looked around. He was standing in a completely circular room that was empty except for one object. In the center of the room was a stone base with a circular depression in it. Straddling the depression was a metal stand. The stand had two levels. The first level consisted of four small circles connected to posts that were horizontally connected to the central column of the stand. The second level consisted of a single central circle suspended over the central column. Directly above the stand was an upside down funnel with a small hole in the top through which David could see the sky. The rest of the room was empty. The walls were rough stone that looked scorched. The entire room was dark and shadowed except for the light coming from the doorway and the beam of light shining through the hole in the ceiling illuminating the stand.

Kira pointed to the stand. "That is the 'quinquetal,' which housed the Imaginator. A little history is in order both to help you understand the problem and also to explain Thane's anger." She walked over to the quinquetal and sat down on the stone base. David moved over to examine the stand but Aradel stayed near the doorway. He seemed nervous about having the door open as if the dome was now much more vulnerable to destruction.

Kira stared up at the hole in the ceiling as she organized her thoughts and then began. "The actual records concerning the Imaginator are very sparse. The earliest writings appear to be references to oral histories about the six treasures of Remin."

"There are only five holders on the stand." David was nothing, if not observant.

Kira pointed at the depression. "The spectrum stone resided in this depression. The oral histories spoke of a fire in the sky that landed here and covered the world with fire. The lakes rose up in waves and flooded the land. When the floods receded, the land came alive with plants and animals. Fire, water, earth, air. The whole history of Remin is centered on this story."

"It sounds like the Bible in lots of ways," said David, "First there is nothing, then God's power created my world."

"That's an interesting observation," enthused Kira. "I've studied the religious symbolism of the Remin story and noticed the parallels. The fire in the sky is popularly thought to refer to a comet or meteorite that impacted on Remin some two hundred thousand years ago. This is roughly the time that humans appeared in your world."

There was a sudden commotion at the door. "Move along. There's nothing to see here." Aradel was now blocking the entire door but David could look right through him and see a small crowd beginning to gather and trying to peer into the open door of the dome. Obviously, it was unusual for the door to be open and their curiosity had brought them into the square to see what was going on.

Kira glanced at Aradel fondly and continued her tale. "It's unclear when the people of Remin discovered the spectrum stone but about six thousand years ago, stories about the stone began appearing. Pieces of the stone were found to be able to ignite fires, or grow plants much faster and larger than normal. The stone was chipped away and the pieces of the stone were used to accomplish miracles for all the people. Eventually it became obvious that using the stone this way was going to destroy the power because at some point there would be no more of the stone left. The people began searching for a new way to harness the power of the spectrum stone."

"Are you saying that the spectrum stone was only as big as that hole in the base?" asked David, pointing at the depression.

Kira nodded. "Yes, by the time the people came up with the Imaginator, the stone was only as big as a large melon. We have never been able to measure any decrease in the output of spectrum from the stone so we currently believe that the stone's power is self-sustaining and can't be exhausted. So the size of the stone does not seem to be a factor. It's a moot point really. The stone is a one-of-a-kind object. Many archaeological expeditions have searched for pieces of the stone and none has ever been found."

"I hope she move this story along. We need to get moving before it's too late." Houdin was becoming impatient again.

"I want to hear it. Don't you think I deserve to know the whole story before we leave?" said David.

"Yes, of course. It's just that with my continuing growth, I'm afraid that it's possible that we won't be able to complete this attempt against Thane before the curse runs its course and I die again. I'll start all over again in a different place. I doubt you'll be able to find me and it's doubtful I could find you in time. I could get lucky and be within flying distance but by the time I found you my time would be up. No, this is by far my best chance to reverse this curse and retrieve the Imaginator. I don't want to waste it."

David sympathized with Houdin's plight but he had to hear the story and after a few more minutes of discussion, Houdin agreed.

Kira had been waiting while David had his discussion with Houdin. It was all a little confusing. David's eyes would glaze over as he talked with Houdin but Kira couldn't hear the conversation. David would always have to summarize once Houdin was done. Sometimes he would verbalize his half of the discussion and Kira could usually fill in Houdin's part based on context. It was like listening to one side of a telephone call. It was a problem but there really wasn't any other solution available. She was sure that David would need this story in order to make the correct decisions on their journey. She added her thoughts to the conversation. "Decisions made without knowledge are always bad decisions. You can't expect David to do what is needed if he doesn't have all the facts. Plus we still need to convince Aradel and he needs all the facts as well."

"Well, hurry it up," Houdin said, but his voice in David's mind was slightly chagrined.

"After much study, it was determined that the real power was not the stone itself but the air around the stone. It's as if the power pours out of the stone and changes the air. There are four different elements to the power as you have by now realized. Fire, water, earth and air. Four crystals were carved from pieces of the stone. Through trial and error the crystals were shaped so that each one extracted one element from the air around the stone." She now pointed to the quinquetal's first level. "The four crystals were placed at this level to concentrate the power of the stone. But now that the stone's power was refined into four separate parts, a way had to be found to bring the powers back together and make it available to the people. That answer resided in the top level of the quinquetal." She pointed upward. "The rainbow prism." David stared up at the top level of the stand.

"The rainbow prism brought the powers of the stone back together. By careful positioning of the four crystals and the prism, the concentrated power of the spectrum stone was made physical in the form of spectrum, which appeared in the air over the prism and was pushed upward through the hole in the dome. The spectrum rises in a steady stream from the dome and is carried over all of Remin by the winds. It is gathered up and used throughout Remin and that is where Thane's anger begins."

At this, Aradel shuffled forward and said bitterly, "I will tell this part of the story for I know it far better than you." He began pacing (if you can imagine a jellyfish pacing) back and forth in front of them. "Remin history since the creation of the rainbow prism is mainly associated with finding uses for the power contained within the spectrum. Developing spells, calculating the percentage of each type of spectrum required for the spell, calibrating wands to dispense the spectrum correctly for each spell. At first all the efforts were for the greater good of Remin. Growing crops, lighting towns and houses, purifying water. But the demand for spectrum soon exceeded the output of the Imaginator. New discoveries were needed."

"The people could not help but notice the dark streamers flowing across the sky. Through experimentation, it was discovered that the streamers contained images, and it was then we realized that we were not alone. There were other worlds. Eventually we realized that the images in the streamers were the dreams of the inhabitants of that other world. We learned that we could use spectrum to influence those dreams. When we did that, we discovered that when spectrum was passed through the streamer it emerged with its power greatly enhanced. Some kind of interaction between the spectrum and the dream altered the spectrum and provided the people of Remin with a solution to their problem. They couldn't increase the output of spectrum from the dome but they could magnify the power of the spectrum that they gathered as it fell to the ground by passing it through the dream streams. Thus was born the art of dreamweaving."

"Years passed and over time we began to notice that the dreams were changing. The images in the dreams showed an increasingly sophisticated culture—cities were built, technologies were developed, and civilizations rose and fell. We learned much about your world, but we could never be sure whether we were truly just observers or whether our manipulations of your dream streams influenced the changes."

David glanced behind Aradel and noticed that many Remin faces were now crammed in the doorway looking and listening as the mano talked. Some were nodding in agreement while others appeared to find the story just as fascinating as David. Either people just naturally loved this story or the history was not well known. David made a mental note to ask Kira about it later. Aradel stopped pacing and looked at the crowd in the doorway. "Don't you people have anything better to do? Go gather whatever spectrum you can find. Help the harvesters in the field." While his voice held a quiver of anger in it, there was a hint of amusement in his chastising tone.

Aradel continued. "But we were blind to the real problems that spectrum caused. Remin is totally dependant on spectrum. We can't live without it. Thane recognized this and his hatred for the dependency grew day by day."

"History shows that we lived without spectrum for thousands of years. When spectrum was first discovered, it was seen only as a way to make things easier and do things that we couldn't do before. But the easy thing is not always the right thing and in this, I still agree with Thane. Remin needs to find a way to break the hold that spectrum has on our society. We need to learn to do for ourselves without the artificial aid that we derive from spectrum. Our life will be harder but more satisfying. Thane began preaching this idea to anyone who would listen." Aradel concluded bitterly, "Folin and I listened."

"But what about my world? Thane doesn't seem to care how his ideas affect my world," David said.

"Thane recognized that his ideas were radical and that they affected your world, which spectrum was affecting without your knowledge. We perceived that human health had come to depend on the changes we make to the dream streams, but Thane's loyalties were with Remin. If Remin broke the cycle and your world suffered, so be it. It was just a necessary evil to Thane's way of thinking. Remin was the important thing. Let other worlds adapt themselves. Most people rejected Thane's ideas but some like Folin and myself saw the logic in it. We wanted what was best for Remin, and Thane convinced us that removing spectrum from our lives was the answer."

Now it was Kira's turn to interrupt. "He must have realized that removing spectrum from our daily lives in such an abrupt manner would have disastrous results, as we couldn't adapt fast enough, either."

Aradel bowed which David took to be nodding. "That's true. I think Thane's original idea was to just remove spectrum from everyday life for a short time so that we could start to see what he saw, but once he go his hands on the Imaginator, his goals changed. When he came to us with his plan, I tried to talk him out of it. To me it seemed too radical. But Folin idolized Thane and believed with all his heart that this was the right thing to do."

"The problem that Thane confronted was the toxic nature of the air around the Imaginator. Once the crystals were in place the concentrated power in the air above the crystals was found to destroy the body's cellular structure. Anyone inside the Imaginator dome for more than a couple of seconds would die. Hundreds of people died when the Imaginator was first constructed. They believed that Remin would benefit from the Imaginator and they sacrificed themselves by entering the dome and working as long as they could to align the crystals and the prism, and make minute adjustments to the quinquetal. That's the main reason why the dome was never guarded. No sane person would attempt to enter the dome. Death was a certainty."

"Thane convinced Folin that the healing amulet would protect him inside the dome. Folin entered the dome and took the spectrum stone, the power crystals and the rainbow prism and gave them to Thane. The healing amulet could not reverse the damage caused by being so close to the stone. The amulet was destroyed and Folin sickened and died a horrible death, betrayed by the man he idolized. When Thane saw that Folin was dying, it seemed that something snapped inside him. He started laughing in that gravelly harsh voice, and it seemed he couldn't stop. He never even said he was sorry."

Tears began to flow out of Aradel's many eyes, creating a cascade of water on the ground around the mano. Aradel sobbed for a moment and then stopped with a sudden snort. His voice grew hard again. "I can never forgive Thane for killing my brother. Telling this story again had made me see how important it is to stop Thane. I still believe that he is right about our self-induced dependency on the Imaginator and that we should find a way to live without the power of spectrum. But not this way. Thane will destroy Remin instead of saving it. I will accompany you." Kira was crying too and David could hear Houdin sobbing as well.

Kira and David moved toward the door and pushed through the crowd still gathered at the entrance to the dome. Aradel followed them out and closed the door behind him. David heard the soft click of the door locking as Aradel pushed it shut. Aradel picked up his weapons, and then moved off through the crowd, talking in soft tones with Kira, who had to stoop down to keep the conversation private.

Kira turned and called back to David, "Aradel and I will gather additional supplies and meet you at the entrance tunnel." She turned and moved off with Aradel without waiting for an answer.

David shrugged and moved through the crowd trying to avoid the stares. He could sense that people from his world were not frequent visitors in Remin. But nobody bothered him. David walked across the central courtyard and seated himself on the side of the fountain. The crowd broke up and returned to their daily routines. Soon the courtyard was almost empty and the dome stood alone in the sunlight. David kicked at the dust with his feet. A few pieces of spectrum glittered on the ground. He turned and watched the water cascading down the side of the fountain. The fountain consisted of several different water creatures shooting streams of water into an overflowing bowl in the center. The sounds of the fountain helped to relax him after hearing the story inside the dome. Houdin started to speak but David needed some private time with his thoughts, so he concentrated on the melding spell and broke the link with the wizard.

David thought hard about everything that Kira and Aradel had told him. Thane does have a good point, he thought. The Imaginator made things easier for Remin but it also made the people lazy. They didn't have to try very hard to accomplish things. They could use spectrum to do their work for them. It was obvious that Thane had accomplished what he set out to do. The people of Remin were now quite aware of how dependent they were on the power of the Imaginator. Thane could return it and things would never be the same. But he didn't return it. Something had changed since Thane had conceived and executed his plan. The Imaginator had corrupted Thane in much the same way that the people of Remin had become seduced by its power.

Soon enough his thoughts were interrupted by the return of Aradel and Kira. They hurried across the courtyard (well, hurried might be a little too strong a word, with Aradel gliding across the courtyard while Kira strolled next to him). Her backpack was now much larger but the extra weight didn't seem to bother her at all. Aradel and Kira both carried walking sticks and Aradel had something like a backpack strapped around his jelly-like body. "Ready to go?" Kira asked crisply.

"Yes," David answered as he stood up. He took his wand out of his pocket and quickly performed the mindmeld again.

Houdin was not happy. "You cut me off," he sulked. David explained his need for quiet thought and Houdin cheered up again. At last they were beginning the journey that could eventually lead to the breaking of the curse. The little caterpillar tried to do another somersault in the cage of the amulet, but was limited by his increasing size.

As they got ready to leave, the water in the fountain suddenly erupted and sprayed them all. With water streaming down his face, David looked at the fountain, but everything looked normal. The stone fish sculptures spouted water in endless streams. But as David looked, he realized that there were two additional statues in the fountain. Fred and Michelle grinned at him, not moving, but shooting streams of water out of their mouths. Except for their color, they appeared to be part of the fountain. David laughed. The two serpents stopped their game and swam over to the group. "Well, what are we going to do?" asked Fred. Michelle was backstroking around the fountain. "This is much nicer than that drafty old tub," she purred.

"We're heading for Lake Istep," said David. Fred frowned. Michelle stopped swimming.

"That's not going be easy," said Michelle.

Fred now looked at the group and said, "It must be serious if you are going to attempt a journey to Lake Istep. Michelle and I have been avoiding that area. I'm not even sure if we can find a way to get there."

"Or even if we want to," interjected Michelle.

"Spoil sport," said Fred, spouting a stream of water in her direction. "Where's your sense of adventure?"

"Well, OK," she answered.

"We'll try to help if we can," they chorused together. With a flip of their tails they disappeared down the fountain drain.

Kira and Aradel started across the courtyard and David followed with Houdin in the amulet. Kira suddenly turned and whistled, and around the corner came a large animal that scampered across the ground and skidded to a halt next to the tall adventurer. Kira smiled, "David, meet Queenie." David grinned and tentatively stuck out his hand in front of Queenie's wolf-like muzzle. "Queenie is a wolfat. She's very friendly." David stared as a long purple tongue began swiping his hand. Queenie had a wolf's face with a lion's ears and mane. The purr that came out of her was a deep but satisfied growl. Kira tapped her thigh with her hand and clucked at Queenie as she began walking away. Queenie followed, loping along next to Kira, darting ahead and then returning to the group.

Kira took the lead with David behind her and Aradel behind David. Kira would be able to move ahead and scout their path. Aradel would guard their rear and be able to protect David and Houdin should any dangers arise.

They soon reached the entrance tunnel. David hadn't gotten a good look at it the night before. Was it really just last night, he thought in amazement. So much has happened. The archway over the tunnel was enormous.

The party quickly moved from the bright sunlight into the shadows of the tunnel and soon enough the only light they had was the flickering of the occasional torch. The tunnel was longer than David had remembered. "I didn't think the lake was this big."

Houdin laughed. "Trust me, it was a long swim."

They walked for almost twenty minutes with only their echoing footsteps and the occasional sound of dripping water to interrupt their thoughts. They stopped only once, when Kira knelt down to look at something lying in the middle of the path. David and Aradel joined her. "Another dead mouse," muttered Houdin as Kira prodded the lifeless ball of fur with her stick. "Remin is not known to have any mice within the city walls. As a matter of fact, until this morning, I have never seen or heard of mice being in the city and now I've seen two. The isolation of the lake means that the only way for animals to get in is through this tunnel.

Kira stood up. "What worries me is that in the past Thane has used small animals to spy for him. I hope there is no connection. I wonder why they are all dead?" She moved off down the tunnel muttering to herself, "Very strange."

Just when David thought the tunnel would never end they were startled to hear a challenge, "Halt, who goes there?" The portal door was looking at them with suspicious eyes.

Houdin sighed, "Oh brother, we're trying to leave the city and it's trying to stop us! What kind of protection is that?" David grinned. Obviously the portal couldn't do anything right in Houdin's eyes.

Kira stepped in front of the portal and declared, "In the name of Kira, I require an exit from the city for myself and my friends."

The portal surveyed the party. Its eyes widened as it looked at David. "Hey, I refused to let you in yesterday. How did you get into the city?"

David straightened his shoulders and said proudly, "I swam the lake and defeated the whirlpools."

"Impossible," the portal declared.

"Nevertheless, it's the truth."

The portal stared at the party as if memorizing their faces and then sighed, "Pass." With a loud rusty creak, the enormous door swung open and the party blinked as the bright sunlight appeared beyond the portal gateway. The party moved quickly out of the shadow of the gateway and the portal door slammed behind them. David found himself back where it all began. Standing at the edge of a cornfield looking down a wide dusty road that vanished into the distance.

7 * SIR HEADS-A-LOT

Kira knelt down and rummaged in her pack, extracting a map, which she quickly unfolded and laid out in front of her. She pointed out various features on the map as she talked. "We are here in the northwest corner of Remin. We need to travel south on this main road until we get to the bridge over the Wolden River. Once we cross the bridge we'll need to make some decisions, but the first part of our trip should be fairly uneventful."

David bounced from foot to foot in anticipation and every few minutes he put his hand on the wand in his pocket as if to reassure himself that it was still there.

Kira folded the map again and started off down the road. On the left was the dead cornfield and on the right the stalks of corn towered over David's head and waved in the breeze.

Houdin had a much better view of things from the amulet than when he was sitting in David's ear and right now he sounded distraught. "Ask Kira about the effects of the spectrum shortages."

"Kira, why do the fields look like this?"

Kira, who had been walking quickly ahead of David and Aradel, slowed her pace to let him catch up. Ahead of them Queenie was darting back and forth across the road chasing something that David couldn't see. When David was walking next to her Kira gestured to the dry field. "This is no accident. The council of Remin made the conscious decision to begin conserving spectrum while this crisis continues. So not every torch is kept lit and not every field is farmed." She gestured toward the growing corn, "We still grow plenty of food. Nobody is going hungry…" and here she paused, "yet."

Aradel came up behind David and interrupted, "Another couple of years like this and we will have food shortages."

They continued past the cornfields and several other fields with crops in various stages of growth or decay. Every once in a while David would see people moving in the fields. He guessed that they might be gathering crops and reloading the spectrum containers. The sun was warm and the journey was easy just as Kira had predicted. Kira talked about Remin farming and then began asking David questions about his world. Aradel seemed somewhat familiar with David's world from his experiences as a dreamweaver, but Kira seemed truly astounded by everything that David mentioned.

"You have lights without fire?"

"No, we have fire but we also have light bulbs powered by electricity. A different form of fire, sort of." David scratched his head. It was hard to compare his world with Remin. Two entirely different cultures.

They made good progress on the road but gradually the road began to veer off to the east. Kira, after consulting the map again, led the group into the dried fields so that they could continue on their southward journey.

Walking through the dried stalks, which were waist high on David, soon became tiring. Kira used her machete to hack away at the stalks and clear the path, but that slowed them down even more and exhausted her. They trudged through the stalks for most of the morning and stopped for lunch, where Kira chopped down a large circle of stalks. They sat eating bread and fruit and gathering energy. Kira fed Queenie who bounded off through the stalks after finishing. David lay back and watched the sky above the dead stalks. In addition to the black dream streams dotting the sky he could also see several large birds gliding back and forth over the group. He had the overwhelming sensation that the birds were watching them eat.

He tore his gaze from the circling birds, sat up and began leafing through one of the spell books he had brought from Houdin's study. Houdin helped him practice aiming his wand and then showed him several simple spells. "The key to any spell is focus," said Houdin. "Spells are easy—focus and imagination are the factors that influence how strong the spell is. Spend your time learning to keep your mind totally directed at the spell that you are attempting and you will always succeed."

David worked with the rehydration spell expanding an apple until it was as big as a pumpkin. He then practiced pushing an orange around the field with jets of air from his wand. As Kira and Aradel packed up the remains of the lunch, Queenie began howling frantically off in the distance. David sniffed the air.

"Do you smell smoke?"

Aradel and Kira glanced up with David and saw that the birds had formed a large circle around them and now they could see that each bird carried a magnifying glass.

"Fire!" yelled Aradel in a panicked voice.

They all started to run away from the dark smoke that began to fill the sky in front of them, but found themselves surrounded by crackling flames. The breeze fanned the flames higher, consuming the dead stalks.

Dark smoke rose all around them in great billows and the flames moved closer. They were soon clustered together in the clearing that Kira had made for their lunch. The flames continued to advance on them and the heat began to rise. Kira and David were both trying to protect Aradel, who was cringing and sobbing and searching for a way out before the intense heat dried his jelly-like body.

As they watched the smoke billowing up, David suddenly noticed that the smoke was not following the wind. It swirled together and began to form into the shape of a man. Houdin

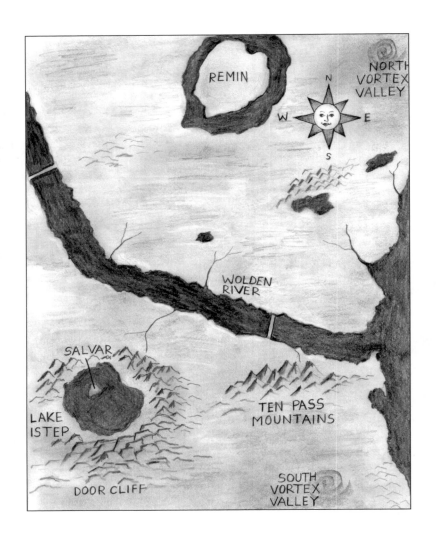

cursed, "Thane! His power is growing. It appears that he already has an army of small animals under his control. What next?"

David was scared. The heat from the flames was closing in on them and Thane's enormous head was towering over them. They couldn't hear anything but the smoky face seemed to be laughing at them, and as they watched, the wind whipped the smoke around and the face dissolved.

David could feel his skin getting hotter and hotter as the cracking flames advanced on them. Kira had her arms wrapped around Aradel and was crouching over him trying to ward off the heat. Queenie continued howling in the distance. Kira yelled above the cracking, "We're going to have to make a run for it. We can't stay here or we'll be roasted."

The mind meld between David and Houdin had broken as the fire consumed all of David's attention. But something in the back of his mind made him reform the meld. As soon as he did he heard Houdin yelling, "Aqueous. Use the aqueous spell. Just imagine a hose spraying water."

David pulled out his wand. It was hard to breathe as the air around them became superheated. He aimed the wand at the flames, imagined a fire hose spraying great streams of water, and shouted, "Aqueous!"

Blue spectrum poured out of the wand and as David watched in astonishment, a stream of water began erupting from his wand to sizzle on the flames, raising great clouds of steam. David focused all his energy on the image of the streaming water. Houdin's voice disappeared as the melding shattered. David directed the water at Aradel who immediately sighed in relief. He then turned back to the flames and began making a path for them through the burning stalks.

Kira saw what David was doing and immediately urged Aradel into motion. She pushed Aradel behind David and crouched over the sobbing mano, as the three of them began rushing forward behind the stream of water flowing from the wand. David's head began to pound as he poured everything he could into the spell.

They scrambled through the burning field and soon left the flames behind them. Queenie appeared out of the haze of smoke and trotted next to Kira, her chest heaving. It was good that they cleared the heat when they did, because David found he couldn't keep the spell going. As he tired, the stream of water turned into a dribble and then stopped. He dropped his arm to his side, completely exhausted.

Kira collapsed next to him, but Aradel continued trying to put more distance between himself and the flames crackling behind them.

After resting for a few moments, Kira shuddered and asked, "How did Thane do that?"

David quickly restored the melding with Houdin. "Thane has always had a great affinity for animals. Even when he was young, it was obvious that animals really like him. Now it appears he has extended that ability to exert some kind of control over mice, and now birds. Maybe even other animals."

Kira grabbed her backpack and hurried after Aradel. David had to run to catch up. They resumed their journey south through the dead fields, often glancing at the sky looking for birds. As the sun began to set they reached the edge of the last field and entered a tree-lined meadow pockmarked with large boulders. They decided to camp for the night in the shadow of a large boulder.

Houdin worked with David on a Dragonium spell that shot a jet of fire out his wand while Aradel gathered fallen tree limbs. David used the spell to start a fire, and they all gathered around it for a quick meal. Queenie paced the edges of the camp while Aradel remained a few steps back from the fire and got out three small cloth squares. "Houdin recommended we bring these. He said you didn't have any trouble with the rehydration spell so if you could do that, we can get some sleep."

David stared at the cloth squares with a puzzled expression on his face. He shrugged and took out his wand and performed the rehydration spell on the first cloth. The cloth expanded and became a big fluffy sleeping bag. David laughed and rehydrated the other two sleeping bags. Then they all curled up to sleep leaving Queenie to guard the camp. Queenie came over and placed her head on Kira's stomach but kept her ears pricked up listening for any unusual noises. David had no trouble falling asleep.

An insistent snuffling and a warm wet tongue introduced David to a new day and he rolled away from Queenie and looked around. The fire was out. Kira and Aradel were already awake and waiting for him. Houdin helped him learn the dehydration spell, which would counter the effects of the rehydration spell. The sleeping bags shrunk back down into compact squares, which Aradel packed away. David restarted the fire and they had sausages, bacon and fruit for breakfast. With each spell, David became a better wizard. His focus increased and his spells worked more frequently. He still made mistakes, like when he was working on picking up objects without touching them and he accidentally floated Kira up into a tree. She climbed down, laughing heartily and started making a path through the boulders.

Soon after starting off, they reached a river. Kira consulted the map and began moving east along the bank of the river until she came to a bridge. Queenie joyfully played in the grass and along the bank of the river as they walked.

As they approached the bridge, Kira stopped suddenly. Kneeling at the edge of the bridge with his back to them was a tall man who was frantically looking for something in the dirt. He sobbed quietly as his fingers scrabbled through the dirt and the river grass along the bank. Kira held the machete in front of her and signaled the other two to stop. Queenie sat at her feet and waited expectantly. The man must have sensed their presence for he suddenly froze and slowly stood up and turned around.

David stared in amazement at the tallest and strangest man he had ever seen. He stood at least eight feet tall. He was wearing a vest that contained hundreds of tiny pockets. His arms were long and completely round like pipes, as were his legs. His body was very square. David felt like he was looking at some kind of robot but scratches and blood on his arms seemed to prove that the tall man was indeed alive. David would have been scared except that the man's face wasn't scary at all. He had been crying and tears streaked the dust on his face, but when he saw them all standing there he broke into the biggest grin that David had ever seen.

"As you can see, I've run into a bit of trouble. Do you think you could help me?"

Kira stepped forward. "What kind of trouble and what kind of help do you need?"

The man indicated the pockets on his vest. "I took a very bad tumble when birds attacked me yesterday evening and I have lost some of my heads. I have been looking for them ever since."

"Your heads?" David exclaimed.

The man fumbled in one of the pockets and held out a tiny object. They all moved forward to look and found themselves looking at a miniature head of a frog. Its eyes were blinking slowly. After staring for a moment, they all looked up at the man.

"My name is Sir Heads-a-lot and I have lost a number of my heads."

Aradel stepped back a little. "The frog head is a neat trick but what's so important about these heads?"

Sir Heads-a-lot smiled. "Please don't be alarmed." He reached up quickly with his hands and twisted his head slightly and David gasped as the head came completely off! As the head came off it shrunk to the size of a button and at the same moment he placed the frog head onto his neck. They all watched in amazement as the frog head grew to match the size of the body. The arms and shoulders of the man transformed into frog legs and one leg placed the button-sized head in a pocket on his vest. They found themselves staring at an eight-foot tall man with a frog's head and front legs. The frog paused and stared at them all for a moment, then winked and reversed the process restoring the original head in a whirl of flailing green. The frog head was placed in a vest pocket.

"That was amazing!"

"Where do you come from?"

"What was the trouble you mentioned?"

The questions flew fast and furious and Sir Heads-a-lot held up his hands good-naturedly. "I will be glad to answer all your questions but first I could really use your help in finding the rest of my heads. I'm missing fourteen heads." He pointed to an area at the edge of the river. "I fell right here. I think that none of the heads are in the river but I can't be entirely sure. If at all possible, I don't want to lose any of them. They are very important to me."

Kira, David, and Aradel all knelt down and began searching. In no time at all Kira found a groundhog head and a cicada head. David was digging right under the bridge when a puppy head suddenly blinked at him from the mud. Aradel waded along the edge of the river with all his eyes staring at the ground. In the shallow water a few feet downriver he spied a weasel head. They spent the next twenty minutes slowly expanding their search and soon had found twelve different heads. The last two heads eluded them.

Just when they were ready to give up, Queenie began growling and digging with her paws in the grass. Kira hurried over and found a button-size snake head hissing at the wolfat. With one more to go they all redoubled their efforts.

David was searching in the grass near the river when Fred and Michelle popped up right next to him. "Looking for something?" crooned Fred. David explained the problem and they both disappeared under the water.

Minutes later Michelle surfaced with a scream. "Get it off, get it off." She was shaking her head violently. Clinging to the serpent was a button-sized turtle head. David waded into the stream trying hard not to laugh and removed the turtle. Sir Heads-a-lot was ecstatic as he pocketed the last head. They all moved to a tree near the bridge, sat down and began to talk.

They all looked expectantly at Sir Heads-a-lot who stood up and began pacing back and forth. "As you may have guessed, I do not come from your world. I come from a place called Inspire which exists on the other side of the vortex."

David asked, "Vortex?"

Aradel pointed back the way they had come. "In the mountains beyond Remin city is a vortex through which the dream streams enter—we assume from your world." He gestured in the other direction and said, "There is an enormous crack in a cliff face where the dream streams exit through another vortex. We believed that the south vortex led to your world, but now it appears that it leads to another world which Sir Heads-a-lot calls Inspire. I can only assume that there are two vortexes in Inspire. One that leads to Remin," he turned to look at David, "and one that enters another world which may or may not be your world."

Sir Heads-a-lot watched Kira fumble in her backpack, withdraw a journal and a pencil and begin scribbling and sketching furiously. He continued, "I was not born this way although my species does have abilities that seem to play a part in my present condition." He stared around at the puzzled faces of his listeners.

"I don't understand."

"How did you get here?"

"How you see me and how I got here are linked," said Sir Heads-a-lot with a smile. "In my world, I am a regen. I have the ability to grow a missing body part. If I lose my arm, I can grow a new one. Even if I lose my head, I can grow a new one. My intelligence is located in an organ in my chest."

Kira stopped writing and stared. Aradel looked as if he didn't believe it and David was open-mouthed in wonder. Queenie seemed totally disinterested and snuffled in the grass nearby. Houdin continued to whisper little asides to David but even he seemed to be having trouble believing the story that was being told.

"I was actually what you would call an entertainer. The heads I carried were plastic heads that could expand to fit over my real head. I had a great show." He paused a little ruefully and added, "If I ever get back I'll have the best show ever." David stared at the pockets on the vest and could see several of them twitching as the heads in them moved around.

"We don't understand the vortex," Sir Heads-a-lot continued. "We have ascertained that the streams that come through the vortex are absorbing something from the air in our world. There is also a belief that the air of my world is nourished by energy being emitted by these streamers although we have little proof of this. We could not help but notice that the streamers have became darker in recent years. Many of our scientists have been analyzing the vortex, but no one has attempted to pass through it before. There are some in my world who believe that the vortex is evil and that we should have nothing to do with it. I traveled to the vortex as a tourist because I was interested in the change in the streamers. I was standing at the fence looking down into the vortex when the ground collapsed under me and I fell into the vortex."

Everyone gasped. Kira said, "No one in Remin has ever attempted to enter the vortexes here, either. The dream streams are too important to the well-being of Remin and we were afraid of disrupting them."

Sir Heads-a-lot nodded. "I thought I would die but I passed through the vortex and found myself here."

Kira now stood up and approached Sir Heads-a-lot. "Yes, but what transformed you into this?" She gestured at the pockets on his vest.

Sir Heads-a-lot scratched his head and grinned. "I was hoping you could tell me. When I found myself here, I also found that all my little plastic heads were alive. Apparently, the trip through the vortex changed me. I tried to reenter the vortex but it appears that I can't go back the way I came. When I tried to go back into the vortex, it was as if a solid wall blocked my path even though I could see the streamers flowing into it. I still didn't understand what was happening but after talking to several people, I was informed that I should travel to Remin city and talk to Kira who might be able to help me."

They all started laughing and Sir Heads-a-lot looked perplexed. "Have I said something funny?"

Kira stepped forward. "Let me introduce our group. The grumpy mano there is Aradel. The little one is named David. The tiny caterpillar on David's necklace is our resident wizard Houdin, who is obviously not himself." She gestured off to the side, "That is Queenie. You already saw Fred and Michelle in the river, and I...am Kira." She bowed and laughed.

Sir Heads-a-lot burst out laughing. "Well, finding you was easier than I expected."

They spent the next hour explaining everything they knew about Thane and how they came to be on this adventure. Sir Heads-a-lot listened with rapt interest.

"Can you help me?" he asked Kira.

Kira shook her head slowly. "We appear to know less about the vortexes than you. When we return to Remin I will do everything I can to help you but I don't have much hope for a quick solution. If we are successful and Houdin is restored, he may be able to help you as well. Passing from Inspire to Remin seems to have had the effect of altering your reality, enhancing your natural biological abilities and breathing life into your plastic heads. I can't explain it but it will be fascinating to study."

Sir Heads-a-lot frowned but nodded with understanding. "Anything you can do would be appreciated. I would like to join you and meet this Thane person."

Kira started to respond but Aradel interrupted, "No, it's dangerous. It's no place for tourists."

Sir Heads-a-lot looked amused. "I think I can carry my own weight around here. I've gotten this far by myself. I only ask for the chance to try. If I find the going too tough, I will be the first to admit it."

Kira said "We can't help him until we get to Thane. Maybe one more person will make the difference."

David stood up and looking up at Sir Heads-a-lot said, "It's a pleasure to meet you and I would love for you to come with us."

Aradel harrumphed and turned away, but Kira said, "Welcome aboard."

They packed up and headed south again. Kira and Queenie scouted ahead, while David walked with Sir Heads-a-lot and Aradel. They crossed the bridge over the river and continued through a landscape of tall grass and boulders. Off in the distance David could see mountaintops poking over the trees in front of them.

8 ✳ DREAMWEAVING

Up until this point their progress had been fairly steady. Aradel and David had found that they walked at about the same pace and Kira was content to forge ahead to scout the path. Queenie scampered around the group as they walked, sometimes running ahead to sniff at something rustling in the tall grass. Several times David saw small animals skulking nearby, or heard the rustle of leaves off to the side of their path, but when he tried to get too close the animals would dart through the underbrush leaving only a faint whisper of their presence. David wondered if they were under Thane's control like the birds in the cornfield. I certainly hope not, he thought.

Their path began to grow steeper as the mountains David had seen over the tree line began to get closer. When they stopped for lunch, Kira pulled out the map, showed David where they were and pointed out their planned route to Lake Istep. "We could have stayed on the road, because it winds its way in this direction, but that would have added several weeks to this journey and I don't think Houdin has that long." She grimaced at the caterpillar hanging around David's neck and then gasped. Houdin was now hanging upside down from the top of the silver cage with his head curled up in a J-shape. David looked and also became alarmed.

"Houdin, you're getting ready to turn into a chrysalis!"

Houdin sighed. "Been here, done this. I can't stop or delay the inevitable. I can only hope that we make good time and that the whole cycle won't complete before we get to Thane."

Kira gestured to the mountains in the distance. "Those are the Tenpass Mountains which are named for the ten mountain passes that go between them. The shortest path to Lake Istep leads up those mountains through one of the passes."

David stared at the map. The mountain range they were approaching consisted of numerous peaks divided by high plateaus. Their path would take them across one of the smaller ones. He stared hard at the mountains ahead of them. The streamers in the sky seemed to gravitate toward these passes and he could see large numbers of streamers flowing between the mountain peaks. Sir Heads-a-lot examined the map and pointed to an area even farther to the east than their planned route.

"I believe that this is the pass I negotiated when I left the vortex."

Kira nodded. "Yes, that would be the most direct route from the vortex but we won't need to travel that far east. Once we get through the pass we'll head south to the foot of Doorcliff and then look for a way to gain entrance to Lake Istep."

"Gain entrance?"

Aradel stared at the mountains and said, "Lake Istep is guarded by the mountains surrounding it as well as various guardians that were installed as protection. The Isle of Salvar in the middle of the lake used to be a monastery where dreamweavers could go to relax and practice their craft. Over the years, as dreamweavers became more adept and the power of the spectrum grew stronger, the monastery was visited less and less and eventually fell into disuse."

Houdin suddenly intruded in David's mind. "This is

an interesting story but do you think we could discuss this while we're moving? I'm not getting any younger here!"

Kira and Aradel packed up and they were soon walking again. The boulders around them grew larger and larger as they continued to head southeast; the path grew steeper and the air became cooler. Aradel unpacked a fur coat, which was very light, but with a trace of a grin he put it on and said, "Very warm." He offered a blanket to David but David turned it down with a matching grin.

"I'm naturally warm. It will have to get a lot cooler than this before I need that blanket."

As the sun began to set they reached the foot of the mountains. In front of them was a rough set of steps cut into the mountain and leading upward into the darkness. They set up camp quickly. Aradel gave Sir Heads-a-lot the blanket for warmth, while David started the fire and prepared the sleeping bags. Queenie came back and curled up with Kira.

After a very quick meal Houdin tried to interest David in some more lessons but David was so tired he begged off, curled up, and was asleep in seconds. Only a soft flap of wings and the scrabbling sounds of little animals moving through the gravel and the grass broke the silence that descended over the camp.

The next morning they broke camp early and started up the steps. David felt energized after a good sleep which was again undisturbed by bad dreams, and climbed steadily over the broken steps. Sir Heads-a-lot was taking the steps two at a time and Kira climbed with Queenie's toenails clicking along next to her. Aradel's climb was the easiest because he was able to ooze his way up the steps with no appearance of effort.

While they climbed, Houdin began working with David again on spells. They practiced the Arcticus spell, which turned into a big game. David aimed blasts of cold air at water droplets coming from the snowmelt above them, turning the droplets into ice that rattled on the rocks like hail.

As they climbed, David began to notice a muted humming sound that grew louder the higher they went. David looked up and gasped. The dream streamers were soaring overhead in great clumps and they were now close enough to see details that had not been visible from a distance. David could see that the streamers were not entirely black. They were shades of gray and black with patches of white. He stared upward in awe at the roiling mass of streamers and then he noticed that the air around them was glittering with spectrum. Aradel noticed David's amazement and moved up to walk next to him.

"Don't be too amazed. I've worked with these streamers most of my life and the excitement wears off quickly." His tone was weary and bitter.

David wasn't even aware of the effort it was taking to climb the stairs. His attention was now focused entirely on the streamers above him. "Can you tell me about them?"

Aradel sighed as he squelched up another step. He reached out to brush stray flecks of spectrum from David shoulders. He stared at the glittering dust that was sticking to his hand (or what passed for a hand on a jellyfish man). "All right. I was as interested as you are now when I was your age."

They suddenly came upon Kira and Sir Heads-a-lot sitting on the steps next to a small pool of snowmelt, eating fruit and talking. Queenie sat on the steps beside Kira. David sat down on the steps and Aradel oozed into a relaxed state next to him. David took a piece of fruit and listened to the melting water dripping into the pool next to him.

Aradel looked at the streamers humming and whizzing by over their heads. "Each streamer is a unique thought generated by a sleeping person in your world. The color of the streamer reflects the type of dream being formed. The dark streamers are what you would call a nightmare. A white streamer would be filled with happy thoughts and stories, but as you can see," he waved an arm vaguely upward, "there are almost no white streamers and very few light gray streamers. Almost every dream that is flowing over these mountains is tinged with darkness. Thane's power now is almost impossible to imagine."

"How can Thane be affecting these streamers? He's not here."

"I think I can answer that," interrupted Houdin. David stopped Aradel while he listened to the wizard.

"I can't be sure but I can make a pretty good guess from my previous encounter with him. Thane is seeding the atmosphere with spectrum. He is collecting spectrum from somewhere and basically scattering dark thoughts through the skies of Remin. When the streamers touch this spectrum they absorb some of the emotion Thane imparted on them. I'm not sure where Thane is getting the spectrum. Maybe he collected and stored it a long time before he took the Imaginator. It's a fairly simple spell to push the spectrum up into the jet stream that envelops Remin."

The water in the pool began quivering like Jello and two icicles rose out of the pool. Fred and Michelle were frozen solid inside the pieces of ice. David scrambled over to the pool but as he frantically tried to grab the floating ice, it began to crackle and split, then exploded, showering everybody with shards of ice. Fred and Michelle both bowed, "Ta-da!" Fred turned to Michelle. "Man, it's cold up here."

Michelle replied, "How cold is it?"

Fred said, "It's so cold, I can't feel my toes."

Michelle giggled, "Maybe that's because you don't have any toes." They both keeled over laughing.

"How did you get up here?"

"Well it wasn't easy," shivered Michelle.

Houdin's worried thoughts interrupted David's mind. "I wish they hadn't followed us. I don't want to risk any more lives than we already are."

David relayed the message. Fred and Michelle both looked hurt. "We just want to be a part of this quest."

Houdin sighed with resignation. "Well, if they really

want to help, send them to scout ahead and see if they can find a good path to Lake Istep, but tell them not to let any of Thane's birds or mice see them. We want them to be safe."

David relayed the message, and Fred and Michelle both stopped frowning, broke into big grins, and disappeared in the pool, leaving only the ripples in the water to show that they had even been there.

Kira stood up and dusted off her pants. "We better get going. I'm sure the guild master won't have any trouble letting us through the pass. Hopefully we can refill David's spectrum sacks here as well. The spectrum that Houdin had is old and could use some recharging. Fresh spectrum might be just the thing when and if we finally find Thane."

David glanced down at the four sacks he was carrying. He had used quite a bit of the water spectrum and the fire spectrum during their nightly camps and their escape from the fire. His air and earth sacks were about half empty.

"Hurry up David!"

He glanced upward and saw that Kira, Aradel and Sir Heads-a-lot were already moving on the steps again. He hurried to catch up and Aradel oozed to his side again so they could continue to talk.

"How do the…the weavers affect the streamers?"

Aradel almost chuckled. "Ah, well that's the trick. You'll see when we get to the pass. The guild members select streams, read them with dream spools and enhance the images using spectrum. It's hard to explain. It's much easier to see, and with your talent for imagery it might be possible to let you try it yourself."

"That would be awesome!" enthused David. "How will I know if I do it right?"

"You'll see." Aradel decided he had said enough and moved back a bit as they continued upward.

David was left alone with his thoughts. He looked at the angry black streamers above him. I can almost touch them, he thought. My parents' dreams could be right there, and they are not good dreams. His mood soured as he thought about all the harm that Thane was doing. And the worst thing is that he knows he's doing it and doesn't care. He was so wrapped up in his thoughts that he wasn't paying any attention and ran smack into Sir Heads-a-lot, who had stopped at the top of the stairs. "I'm sorry," David said, as he stepped around Sir Heads-a-lot to get a better look. When he reached the top of the stairs, his mouth fell open.

Aradel slid up to him. "Impressive, isn't it?"

They were standing at the edge of a large flat plain nestled between two mountains. It stretched off into the distance, disappearing behind a curtain of mist. They were at the top of a large stone wall looking down into a vast bowl surrounded by the towering mountain cliffs. Mist swirled around the craggy peaks. The air around them glittered with eddies of spectrum in constant motion from the stiff breeze whistling over their heads. The dream streams cast undulating shadows on the ground causing a strobe light effect, and the humming that came from them was almost deafening.

David kept blinking as he tried to absorb what he was seeing. People filled the pass from end to end. Thousands of bright electrical flashes, which David recognized as spectrum energy, arced from the ground into the sky and connected with the streamers as they wafted through the air. The glittering spectrum in the air mingled with the mist and created hundreds of tiny rainbows, which appeared and disappeared with the rapidly changing energy patterns. As he tried to absorb all this, he heard a clanking sound and, glancing down the stone wall, he saw a granite platform ascending with a solitary figure standing in the middle and staring upward. Kira, recognizing that this was Aradel's domain, gestured for him to step forward which he reluctantly did. As he did so, he reached into his coat and withdrew a stone wand topped with a glass spool, which he held in front of him stiffly as he waited for the stone platform to reach their position.

David whispered to Kira, "What's happening?"

Kira kept staring straight ahead but she replied out of the corner of her mouth, "The guild master is coming."

The head of the guild master appeared as the platform rose up and stopped at the top of the wall. David found himself staring at the bear-like features of the master and thought to himself, they all look approximately the same but only Thane looks scary. I wonder why that is? Kira and Houdin and even this master look almost cuddly but Thane looks menacing. It must be the eyes.

The eyes that were staring at them now were bright but puzzled. The master was staring at Aradel's spool and raised her hands as if in prayer as a sign of acknowledgement.

"Welcome weaver. I am the guild master here. My name is Orionar. You bring us news?"

Aradel lowered the spool. "I am Aradel and I bring news and visitors. We desire to traverse the pass as rapidly as possible but we will stay long enough to tell you our tale and take with us any tales you may wish to share." This seemed to end the formal introduction, for the guild master dropped her hands and laughed heartily, turning to look at Sir Heads-a-lot.

"I am eager to hear your tales and I have one of my own. Come." She gestured them onto the platform. They stepped onto the platform and at a signal from the guild master the platform rapidly descended. The loud humming of the streamers decreased, only to be replaced by the hubbub of the thousands of weavers practicing their craft. Orionar disembarked from the platform and beckoned the group over to a cave carved into the cliff face. David caught a quick glimpse of the crowd and saw mano, the bear-like Remin, and other creatures that he didn't recognize.

They entered the cave and David noticed right away that there was no shortage of spectrum here. The cave was brightly lit by hundreds of torches. It resembled the Remin Plaza: a huge round cave with many smaller cave entrances on the periphery.

Orionar moved into one of the smaller caves and they found themselves in a room dominated by a stone table and chairs. The room was warm so Aradel removed his coat and everyone sat down. The guild master crossed her hands in front of her and waited expectantly.

Kira recounted Houdin's fall and David picked up the story with Houdin's rediscovery. The story went back and forth among the entire group with Sir Heads-a-lot chiming in with his story again until finally the tale wound up at the table where they all sat.

Orionar had been wide-eyed through the entire story. She stood up. "Let us begin traversing the pass and I will tell my tale as we walk. When we reach the south wall, we can replenish your supplies." She turned to a mano that had entered the room, gave some instructions and then moved toward the cave entrance.

They all clustered around her as they walked out of the cave. She led them over to a carved marble platform resting on a wide path that ran along the cliff wall. As they stepped on the platform David could see a jelly like substance oozing from under the platform. Two mano stood on the back of the platform with long wooden oars.

Orionar waved her hand. The mano pushed off, and the platform began gliding smoothly down the path. She had to speak loudly to be heard over the din of the weavers and the humming of the streamers overhead. She gestured toward the cave entrances arrayed along the wall. "There are connecting tunnels between all of the passes in these mountains to allow for communications between the guild masters, and the news that reached me two days ago has been quite troubling. Your arrival interrupted a meeting where we were trying to reach a decision on what actions to take."

She stared around at the group and noticed their puzzled faces. "I'm sorry, I should have started with the news. Two days ago, word reached me from Far Pass that the guards at the vortex are encountering some strange things. Birds have attacked the guards; large rocks are being dropped from the upper cliffs in a misguided attempt to block the vortex. Several of these rocks have fallen through the vortex."

Sir Heads-a-lot gasped. "There could be many people injured in Inspire if boulders are unexpectedly arriving through the vortex!"

Orionar nodded sadly. "It's true that we cannot predict the results of this event on the other side of the vortex but we are discussing what we can do to stop these attacks. If Thane is behind these attacks, and your story implies that he is, we must find a way to stop him. We cannot know what awaits this world if the vortex is permanently blocked. When you arrived we were preparing to send messages to Remin City asking for help. Now that you are here, I can make my request in person." The platform moved smoothly down the path. Already they were halfway across the pass.

Kira stared straight ahead. "How far to the vortex?"

Aradel growled under his breath—he knew what that question meant. They were going to diverge from their goal.

Orionar talked to the mano that were guiding the platform and moments later the platform glided to a halt. She stepped off the platform and the others followed. She pointed to a brightly lit cave entrance across the pass. "That tunnel will take you to Far Pass which leads directly to the vortex."

She began crossing the plain. Aradel rushed to catch up with her and spoke to her in low tones as they moved through the crowd. Orionar stopped and turned to David. "Aradel tells me that you show great promise as a wizard. Would you like to try your hand at weaving? Aradel can assist you."

David was surprised. Aradel had mentioned this but he had not expected to be given the opportunity to try. He fumbled in his jacket and removed his wand and the glass spool that Houdin had given him. "Yes, I would like to try." His smile stretched from ear to ear. Following Aradel's instructions he fitted the spool onto his wand. Aradel removed his own wand and spool.

"I'm not so sure this is a good idea," said Houdin. "Dream images can be unexpected and hard to handle."

"But I want to try. I want to see what it's like. Maybe it will help me understand Thane."

Houdin reluctantly agreed. Aradel discussed the procedure with David, then stepped aside and watched.

David stared upward at the streamers flowing over his head. I need to find a light gray or a white one. He chose a light gray one. Houdin was whispering to him. "Focus...focus..." David focused on the streamer and rotated the spool with his hand.

Immediately the spool began spinning by itself and a sputtering stream of spectrum power arced from his wand toward the streamer, but as David watched and tried to direct the stream, it vanished. David watched, disappointed as the streamer passed over his head. A powerful stream of spectrum arced up behind him and captured the streamer, and as quickly as the stream started it ended and the weaver moved on to another streamer.

"What went wrong?"

"You have to let the spool and the spectrum make the connection. You can't force it. It's a very subtle difference. Maybe you're not ready for this."

"Let me try one more time."

David waited and watched for a while as the streamers streaked by. Please give me a white one. As if in answer to his desire a billowing white streamer streaked toward him. Again he set the spool spinning and this time he divided his attention between the spool, the spectrum and the streamer. The power arched from his wand to the streamer and this time it connected and the image of a snowman without a face appeared. David quickly drew the image of a smiling face on the blank white head and added a tall black glittery top hat. He sent the image to the streamer, and as the streamer passed over his head the arc of power dissipated and a light shower of spectrum began fluttering to the ground and wafting away above him. He turned delightedly to Aradel. "I did it. I think. I drew a snowman face!"

Aradel nodded and Orionar smiled. "You might make a good weaver," she said.

"Let me try another one."

Kira had been standing at the edge of the path. "We need to get moving."

"Please. Just one more."

Sir Heads-a-lot said to Kira, "Come on. It doesn't take long. Let him try again." Kira stepped back and crossed her arms impatiently but she was smiling.

David readied himself and started looking for a light-colored streamer. He spotted one, started the spool spinning and watched as the energy of his wand sought out the streamer but as he watched, the line between his wand and the streamer altered course and latched onto a pitch-black streamer. He involuntarily looked into the spool and watched in horror as Thane's face leered up at him. As quickly as the face appeared it vanished in a puff of black smoke as the connection was broken and the streamer soared upward and vanished in the mist. David turned to look at Aradel who was staring at the spool with a look of horror on his face.

"Did you see him? Thane!"

Aradel nodded but continued to stare. "Yes, I saw him. I don't understand how he's tracking us or how he managed to bring his image into your spool. It's inconceivable yet clearly he has mastered spectrum power in Remin. He may be the most dangerous man in Remin, Inspire, or Earth." Aradel shuddered. Kira was now pushing on David's shoulder.

"We have to hurry."

They moved toward the tunnel entrance. Several mano were waiting for them. One carried several bags of spectrum, which David used to refill his sacks. He also reloaded his wand. Aradel, Kira and Sir Heads-a-lot refilled their sacks with food and supplies from the other mano. Houdin was muttering in David's ear.

"I was worried about what you would see in a dark streamer but I never thought that Thane could find a way to do what he did. We're in more trouble than I ever imagined."

David shivered in the cool air. They moved into the tunnel to begin their journey to Far Pass. Maybe this is too hard for me. Maybe I should go home.

9 ✳ THE EDGE OF THE WORLD

Torches lit the tunnel with a flickering glow as they traveled through the mountain. Soon after they started off, the tunnel narrowed and Sir Heads-a-lot had to stoop to avoid hitting his head. He remedied that quickly by switching heads, which David watched in undisguised amazement. Any doubts that he had about continuing on this journey disappeared in an instant. The transformation was like watching a candle melt into another shape. As soon as the new head was in place, Sir Heads-a-lot began sprouting fur. This time his whole body was transformed instead of just his arms, shoulders and head, and in moments David was walking next to a sleek mountain lion, who loped easily down the tunnel.

Queenie's howling barks could be heard echoing up and down the tunnel as she ran on ahead and Kira walked with her machete held up protectively and her head almost brushing the roof.

David strengthened his focus on the melding with Houdin. "Why would Thane want to block or destroy the vortex? If he is making use of the streamers himself it doesn't make any sense to destroy them."

"I don't believe Thane is entirely sane anymore. His possession of the spectrum stone has blinded him to his original goal. I believe that at first he thought he was going to help

119

Remin rediscover itself, but the power has driven him mad. He is no longer himself."

David walked on, pondering Thane's actions and their own attempt to thwart him. We are weak against him but our desire to succeed is strong. Can we be strong enough to make a difference? I hope so, he thought. He turned his attention to the torches and marveled at the power of the fire spectrum, which kept them lit. And as he watched the torches he suddenly felt a cold wind blast down the tunnel and extinguish the lights plunging them into total darkness.

David froze. He felt the panic growing, paralyzing him, until Houdin's voice in his mind steadied him. "Use your wand and relight the torch."

David fumbled for his wand and began feeling along the wall for the next torch. The darkness closed in around him and his hands felt clammy and cold. He felt an animal brush against his leg as it ran by him. His fear began to rise. Finally, his fingers touched a torch and he lit it with his wand. Sir Heads-a-lot's eyes reflected the dim torchlight and his lion head swayed back and forth.

The lion spoke, "Something is coming." A fluttering noise began growing in the tunnel behind them and as David watched in horror a huge black bat soared out of the darkness and latched onto the mountain lion's neck. Behind the bat came hundred of other bats.

Kira yelled, "Run!"

They all broke into a stumbling run but soon found that they outran the light from the single torch and were in darkness again. The bats were all around them. David could hear the clang of Kira's machete and Aradel's sword as they swung and hit the rock walls surrounding them. He waved his arms and knocked a fluttering bat to the ground. Houdin was now yelling, "We need light to fight; focus on a bright light and try the Flourescium spell."

David tried to calm himself down and focus and in moments he muttered the spell and had to shield his eyes as his wand burst into a blinding flash of silver and red spectrum that illuminated the dark tunnel. The dark mass of bats was all around them, but the light allowed Kira and Aradel to effectively fight.

Sir Heads-a-lot transformed into a hawk and brought down several of the bats, leaving them stunned on the floor of the tunnel. David noticed that the flight of the hawk was very erratic. Several times Sir Heads-a-lot could be seen tumbling to the ground or bouncing off a wall.

They continued to fight but they weren't making much progress. The bats kept coming and no matter how many were knocked down or stunned, more came to surround the group. They were now backing down the tunnel with Kira and Aradel in front of David and Sir Heads-a-lot flying nearby. The cramped tunnel became increasingly claustrophobic and the light from David's wand began to waver as his focus weakened from fear and anxiety.

Houdin said, "This isn't helping us. We need to try something else." He talked quickly, explaining a complicated spell to David. David followed his instructions and stepped in front of Kira and Aradel who redoubled their efforts to protect him. The light from the wand died as he changed spells.

"Marcelium," David said, and the tip of the wand glowed. David traced a square that spanned the entire tunnel, drawing an invisible wall. As he completed the square he shouted "Marceau," and the glowing lines expanded and brightened to form a wall of energy that filled the tunnel. The bats ran into the wall and fell to the ground. Kira and Aradel stunned the rest of the bats that fluttered around them and they quickly retreated down the tunnel.

"How long will that wall stay there?" panted David.

"Not long," said Houdin. "But we should have enough time to put some distance between us and come up with a better defense." They moved as quickly as they could. Sir Heads-a-lot was a mountain lion again, and as they moved away from the glowing wall the darkness of the tunnel descended on them again. And just when David began to relax, the dim glow from the wall vanished as the energy sustaining the barrier frayed and collapsed. The bats were rushing at them again!

"Houdin, what do we do now?" David screamed as the tunnel grew dark again and the loud fluttering of the angry bats swelled. But Houdin was silent. David concentrated on mind-melding with the wizard, but for the first time in a long time he couldn't do it. He could feel the sweat on his face even though the cold breeze was still whistling down the tunnel. He tried to remember the spell that Houdin had just told him for creating a bright light, but in his panic he couldn't find the right word. A bat fluttered by his head. The sounds of battle from his friends began again. David squeezed his wand and a pale glow grew around them. He looked down at the amulet hanging around his neck and gasped. Houdin was gone! In his place was a green chrysalis with gold stripes.

Oh no, he thought, *I'm on my own.* He tried to think of which spell would help them against the bats but there was too much going on around him. Then he had an idea. Bats use sound to navigate. A high-pitched sound might confuse them. He reached into his jacket and fumbled for the glass spool. A bat landed on the back of his neck and he shooed it off with his hand.

Aradel and Kira were cursing and panting in the darkness ahead of him. He pulled the amulet off the chain, put it in his pocket and then ran the chain through the spool. The cold wind was increasing. The frenzy of the bats increased. He knelt down and began to whip the spool around his head in a tight circle. As he increased the speed the wind began to whistle through the hole in the spool and a high piercing shriek began to echo through the tunnel.

The bats went crazy. They ran into each other, and the walls, and fell, stunned, to the ground. The rest of the bats desperately flew away from the sound and in seconds the sounds of the bats faded away. The energy wall had cut off the cold wind that had been blasting down the tunnel, and as suddenly as the attack had started, it stopped. The torches in the tunnel burst into light again.

David stopped the spinning spool, put it back into his pocket and put the amulet back around his neck. Kira and Aradel slumped, panting heavily, against the tunnel walls but Kira was staring at him with approval. Sir Heads-a-lot, in his lion form, was licking his paws and looking very disheveled.

Kira gasped, "How is he tracking us?"

Aradel said, "Maybe it's David. He's different. Maybe Thane sees him differently and tracks us using David. He found David in Houdin's bathroom and also the weaver plain. The fire attack may also have been centered on David."

They all observed the tiny green chrysalis, and Kira and Aradel looked meaningfully at each other. David knew they were wondering how they were going to continue without the wizard's guidance and support. "If Thane can track me, maybe I should go back. I'm not much good without Houdin to tell me what to do, and you'll make better time without me, anyway."

Kira and Aradel both argued against that reaction. "We don't know if Aradel is right. It's just a theory. Beside, we need you and we need to try and help Houdin. We couldn't have defeated the bats without you, and you did that all by yourself, with no help from Houdin." Kira smiled fondly at David and wrapped her arms around his shoulders. "Come on. It's got to be harder for Thane if we keep moving."

They started down the tunnel again and for the next couple of hours they were able to walk in silence with no other attacks. The tunnel widened and they found themselves in a large cavern festooned with large stalactites and stalagmites. A small lake occupied one corner of the cavern and they all gathered together and sat down to rest and eat. Sir Heads-a-lot returned to his normal form while sitting on the cavern floor, explaining that the transformations required a vast amount of energy and focus. David noticed that there were deep scratches on the backs of his hands.

"I noticed that when you were a hawk you seemed to have a lot of trouble flying. Are you hurt?" asked David.

Sir Heads-a-lot smiled ruefully. "Well, I quickly found out that transforming into a bird is a lot easier than actually flying like a bird. I think it has something to do with my weight. I'm still an eight-foot regen in a different body, so my mass is denser and thus heavier. I was going to fly to Remin City until I found this out through trial and error. I got a lot of bumps and bruises to prove it." He laughed. "I don't fly unless I have to and then I choose the biggest birds that I can, like hawks, eagles, and vultures."

David found his attention drawn to the lake. The water in the lake looked like a piece of glass. They all watched in amusement as the surface rippled and Fred and Michelle popped up.

"This is more like it: a nice, quiet lake. We ought to stay here a while."

David leaned over the lake and the two grinning serpents swam up to him.

"I'm glad to see you again." They gently touched his hand.

Fred's smile vanished as he looked at the tired group. "It looks like Thane is wearing you down."

As soon as he said it, Kira and Aradel both straightened up and prepared to continue on to Far Pass. Sir Heads-a-lot returned to the mountain lion form and with a quick goodbye to the serpents, they started off. Fred and Michelle waved their little arms. "We'll see you on the other side."

It was now very late in the day. No one wanted to stay in the tunnels overnight so they moved on at a rapid pace. Just when David began to despair that they would never reach the end, the tunnel began to widen again, and as exhaustion overtook the group they reached Far Pass. The guild master here quickly found them a room and with a whispered word of thanks, they all collapsed and slept fitfully through the rest of the night.

"David, quickly, we have to go." David stared up into Kira's anxious face. "The guild master is calling us."

Instantly awake, David hurried to get ready. Aradel, Sir Heads-a-lot and Kira rustled around gathering their supplies. Queenie opened one eye and sleepily watched the activity. As they left the room, the wolfat ambled to her feet and followed.

They mounted a platform that took them to the south end of Far Pass. Even though David was now comfortable with the weaving activity going on around him, he still found it fascinating. I hope I get another chance to try it again, he thought, but as he looked up at the many black streamers overhead he decided not to ask.

The guild master was having a very concerned conversation with Kira and Aradel and as they took the elevator platform up to the top of the south wall, David could see why. From the top of the wall they could look down the mountain into a narrow valley. Thousands of dream streamers were flowing from the mountain passes right into the valley. The streamers over their heads were swooping lazily over the end of the pass and plunging downward toward the unseen vortex.

The guild master pointed into the valley. "When the animal attacks began I sent a group of mano into the valley to guard the vortex. The attacks stopped but Thane actually attempted an attack himself. The mano reported that he appeared at the valley entrance, but when he saw the number of mano near the vortex, he retreated."

"So Thane is here!" Kira hissed.

The guild master shook his head. "No, we have searched the valley and have found no trace of him."

Aradel pointed to a cluster of smaller mountains. "Lake Istep is behind those mountains. From here we can descend into the valley to investigate the guild master's story and then proceed toward the Lake."

The guild master handed a piece of paper to Aradel. "This can be used to gain entrance to the valley. Show this to the guards and they will let you pass." They thanked the guild master and began to scramble down the rocky path that led down the mountain toward the valley.

Going down the mountain proved to be much easier than climbing up. Aradel just slid over the uneven path. Several times he allowed David to hitch a ride by extending two globs into arms for David to hold onto while skating on the residual jelly that trailed behind. Sir Heads-a-lot transformed into a mountain goat and clambered down the rocky scree. Kira and Queenie recklessly skidded down the path scattering stones and pebbles as they went.

In a matter of hours they reached the bottom of the mountain. They paused to rest and drink water and then started off down a well-used path toward the valley. The rocky ground quickly changed to scrub grass as they hurried on toward the valley. It wasn't hard to stay on course with the vast number of streamers all heading in the same direction.

As they approached the head of the valley they stopped for lunch near a small stream, which appeared to follow the path down toward the vortex. Aradel stood guard as they ate. From here they could see that several mano were stalking the entrance to the valley.

David was looking forward to seeing the vortex. He couldn't imagine all the streamers over his head all destined for the same point. Fred and Michelle appeared as they finished their lunch. They began skipping stones in the stream. Kira walked over to the two playful serpents. "If you want to help, why don't you scout on ahead and let us know what we can expect when we reach the valley." Fred and Michelle both snapped to attention and saluted.

"Aye, aye captain. Your wish is our command." They started off down the stream zigzagging and moving stealthily with just their eyes sticking out of the water like alligators.

David spent a good part of the lunch trying to talk to Houdin. It was useless and finally he gave up and walked over to Aradel. "What can we do? Houdin can't help and we have very few weapons."

Aradel sighed, "We can make better decisions if we are informed. We have to find out what the guards know. Maybe we can figure out what Thane hopes to gain by blocking the vortex. I certainly can't understand his goal right now."

Fred and Michelle appeared again. They snapped to attention. "Reporting as requested, captain!"

They all gathered around the two serpents. "Well, if Thane attacks by water it will be easy for him. The mano don't seem to care about the stream."

Kira said impatiently, "Thane is bigger than this stream. Of course he's not going to use the stream."

Fred was indignant. "You asked for a report and now you don't like what we saw."

Kira looked embarrassed. "I'm sorry, go on."

Michelle looked satisfied but Fred still looked put out. Michelle said, "Four very nervous mano are at the entrance to the valley and four more are near the vortex. No sign of Thane."

Kira thanked them for their report and the group prepared to continue. As they started down into the valley, a shadow suddenly passed over David. He looked up and cried out, "Kira! Aradel! Thane is coming!"

They all turned to see a man being held up by two large birds soaring toward the valley. The mano in the valley had seen Thane as well and now moved forward with spears to try to strike the evil weaver. Their spears all fell short of the mark.

Kira broke into a run and they all quickly followed. "We have to help if we can," she panted. They raced into the valley.

Thane had soared right over the heads of the mano and disappeared into the shadows. The mano ran after him.

It took Kira's group almost twenty minutes to reach the entrance to the valley and, as they raced into the shadows, they saw Thane above them again heading toward the mountains encircling Lake Istep. Kira stopped and had Queenie stand guard for them at the entrance, then the rest of the group started running again. As they pelted across the valley floor, the humming of the streamers overhead was almost deafening. David could see the mano up ahead but they weren't moving. They ran up to the first mano. Aradel cried out and began pounding on the mano with the back of his sword. The mano was frozen solid!

"We must find out what Thane did to the vortex," shouted Kira. They hurried forward, passing more of the mano, all solidly encased in ice. The valley curved slightly, and the vortex loomed in front of them. They skidded to a halt in amazement.

The valley ended in a sheer stone cliff with a giant crack in it. The vortex occupied the entire cliff face and towered over their heads. It appeared to be made of golden smoke, which spun gently in the crack, around a dark purple center. Starting from the edge and spiraling toward the center were the smoke-like dream streamers.

It wasn't hard to see what Thane had done. An enormous energy wall stood in front of the cliff face. The streamers flowing down the valley ran into the energy wall and vanished with a loud shriek. The noise was deafening and David covered his ears with his hands.

Kira walked carefully up to the wall and touched it tentatively with her walking stick. The stick rebounded and clattered to the ground. Kira shook her numb hand and stared back at Aradel, David and Sir Heads-a-lot.

"We have to stop this," cried Sir Heads-a-lot. Even as they watched they saw the last of the streamers behind the energy wall vanish into the vortex. Now the vortex continued to revolve but it was empty of streamers. "The loss of the streamers will affect my world."

They all stared at the energy wall. "Won't it just break down like the small one in the tunnel?" asked David.

"Well, if Houdin were here, he could give a better answer but my guess is that the size of this wall has some bearing on how long it will last. This one may last days or even weeks," said Kira, bending to retrieve her stick.

Aradel looked at the frozen guards and spoke in a tight voice. "He needs to be stopped. He doesn't care about anybody but himself anymore."

David stared at the energy wall, watching the electric charges as they arced back and forth between the edges of the barrier. He took out his wand while the other three watched him and used it to spray a stream of water on the energy wall. The electricity in the wall stopped its regular pattern and broke up as it sought out the falling water, but as soon as the water was gone the power of the wall leveled out again. David knew he was on to something. "We need a big container that can hold water," he yelled over the piercing sound of the streamers.

Sir Heads-a-lot searched through his pockets and then went to stand halfway between the barrier and the small stream in the valley. He switched heads and they all watched as he transformed into an enormous pitcher plant. His legs and body became a long green vine and his arms became leaves. His head expanded to become an enormous open-ended bulb. At first David was puzzled but Aradel grasped the concept and immediately dragged the bulb over to the stream and filled it with water.

David explained his idea. Kira stood next to the wall with Aradel's sword in one hand and her machete in the other. Aradel began heaving large quantities of water on the upper parts of the barrier using the pitcher plant. Fred and Michelle popped up and began spraying water on the bottom of the wall. The wall sizzled and smoked as the water disrupted the arcing electricity but gravity dragged the water to the ground too quickly to have any permanent effect on the wall.

David stood back and began using the spell Houdin had taught him on the climb up the Tenpass Mountains. Silver spectrum shot out of his wand in an icy blast of air, which he directed at the falling water. The water froze on contact. Aradel, Fred and Michelle threw water at the wall while David directed icy blasts from his wand. Soon the entire energy barrier was coated in a thick layer of ice with the arcs of electricity seeking each other out through the shimmering sheets of frozen water. The edges of the barrier dimmed and David yelled to Kira, "Now!"

Kira threw both weapons with all her might at the center of the icy barrier. The sword and machete struck the center, and the wall shattered into icy shards that rained down on them. As the ice broke the edges of the barrier dimmed even more. Suddenly the barrier could not be sustained, and it collapsed. The shrieking of the streamers vanished to be replaced by the natural hum as the streamers began flowing once more into the vortex.

Kira smiled in satisfaction as she went to retrieve the weapons. Aradel gently placed the pitcher plant on the ground and stood with his hands on his hips staring up at the results of their efforts. The leaves of the plant wrapped around the bulb and very soon Sir Heads-a-lot was standing there, grinning from ear to ear. Fred and Michelle were dancing around in circles, "Yay!"

David now turned to the frozen mano. "Can they survive being frozen, Aradel?"

"They can survive cold better than they can survive heat," said Aradel.

They moved all eight of the mano together around the mano campsite, which they had found near the entrance to the valley. They then gathered as much dead wood and plants as they could find and piled it in the center of the circle of frozen mano. David lit the brush and they watched in silence as the mano began to thaw, creating huge puddles on the ground. Soon large slabs of ice began to fall off of the mano and in short order all eight of them were free from their icy prisons.

They decided to camp with the mano for the evening so they could rest, discuss possible strategies for dealing with Thane if he returned, and trade stories. Despite their eagerness to go after Thane, they all realized that if they didn't rest they would be too exhausted to battle.

Kira called for Queenie who came running. The mano guards set up a rotating watch to protect their guests. The guards shared their food, and the smell of roasted meat was soon wafting over the entire valley. David had three helpings of the meat, which the mano guards called 'pika'. David thought it was delicious and said it tasted a lot like chicken. When he had eaten his fill he prepared his sleeping bag and lay down watching the bright stars visible above the valley. As sleep came over him, he curled up in his sleeping bag and stared at the tiny green chrysalis.

Kira walked over and knelt down. The dying light of the nearby fire flickered in her eyes as she smiled at him. "You are proving yourself to be quite an imaginative wizard even without Houdin's help. You surprise me little one. I am glad to have you with us. You have already struck a blow against Thane and you have helped all our worlds, plus... you have helped the mano guards. Aradel won't forget that and neither will the guards. Sleep well for I am sure that more challenges await us."

David smiled. "I thought before that I should find a way to get back home, but I was wrong. I'm glad to be with you." He looked at the chrysalis again.

Kira said, "Houdin and your parents would be very proud of you."

David smiled again, closed his eyes and murmured, "I know."

10 * THE WRESTLE FIGHT

They all slept late the next day, but as soon as they had eaten they said goodbye to the mano guards and left the valley. Before they left, the guards gave them all the information they had on Lake Istep and the best way to get there.

As soon as they started out Kira noticed paw prints in the soft earth. "It looks like something is tracking us. The prints are similar to those made by baby wolfats, yet not exactly the same." She watched Queenie sniff the tracks and growl. "I hope it isn't more of Thane's creatures . . ." Kira set a steady pace as she discussed their journey to the lake and what she had learned from the guards.

"The big problem," said Kira, "is that we don't know how to get around the safeguards that protect the lake."

"What kind of safeguards?" David almost shouted his question before he realized that the loud hum of the dream streamers was gone as they moved away from the Tenpass Mountains and the vortex.

"Here's where we could really use Houdin. Some of the wizards who came before Houdin placed magical locks in the form of guardians at the entrances to the lake. Thane appears to be able to use birds to bypass the guardians by flying over them. We don't have that luxury. Even at his strongest, Houdin could only fly himself for short distances. It takes incredible concentration and a large amount of spectrum."

The mountains surrounding the lake loomed in front of them with the tops hidden in mist. David stared at the mountains and thought about Houdin. It's lonely, he thought. I miss my conversations with him and everything that he was teaching me. I'll have to keep learning on my own.

When they stopped to rest David spent every spare moment reading the spell books that he had borrowed from Houdin. Every couple of hours he would try to contact Houdin but the chrysalis seemed impenetrable. He practiced simple spells like levitating objects or making them come to him like a magnet. He also read up on complex spells like finding water under the ground and tying his shoelaces without touching them. Aradel and Kira watched as he concentrated so hard he gave himself a headache trying to make a flower bloom. But he made tremendous progress. He found that he was especially good at fire and water spells. Air spells were tougher but earth spells were the toughest.

"Why doesn't this work?" David sighed in exasperation as his attempt to force a flower to bloom failed again.

"Spells which affect living things require you to understand how that particular life interacts with the world around it. I'm sure Houdin could explain it better," said Aradel. "That's a big reason why there are very few wizards in the world. Imagination will only take you so far, after that it takes natural talent and an intense curiosity about the world around you. Houdin had that talent and it appears that you have it as well."

As they got closer and closer to the lake David could see that the mountains were really a series of high cliffs. Kira's map showed that the cliffs completely encircled the lake. It looked to David like the lake was really a crater, a deep depression with high walls. He couldn't see any breaks in the cliffs at all. From time to time a bird would circle them and then fly off toward the cliffs and Aradel would grumble and shake his jelly-like arms at the apparent spies.

They approached the cliffs cautiously, veering off the

natural path and venturing into tall grass, which gave way to a forest of trees. At the edge of the tree line they stopped to rest and eat. Queenie marked several trees and then played fetch with David. Eventually they both tired of the game and sat down to relax in the shade of a large oak. David stared at the dark forest now blocking their way. He wondered what might be lurking in the darkness under the trees. Kira sat and sharpened her machete by sliding it back and forth on a stone, which she carried with her. Aradel marched up and down in front of the forest with an air of impatience and Sir Heads-a-lot sat off to the side practicing head juggling. He smiled at them, "I'm an entertainer, be entertained." He launched into a whole routine involving juggling, gymnastics and head switching. David forgot about his nervousness as he and Kira laughed and clapped at the regen's antics. Only Aradel remained aloof from the frivolity. He continued to pace and stare into the shadows of the trees.

Soon enough they were ready. Sir Heads-a-lot placed a deer head on his shoulders and soon stood with them as a magnificent stag. Kira sighted the cliffs over the trees in order to choose their direction and then called for the wolfat. For once Queenie did not rush ahead but rather she stayed at Kira's side as she advanced into the trees, using her machete to hack a path for them when the undergrowth became too thick.

"At least those pesky birds won't be able to track us so easily," said Aradel as he stared at the dense canopy of trees above them.

A loud commotion pierced the silence and a frantic rustling began in a tree behind them. They turned and watched as a shower of feathers cascaded out of the air. "I wonder what happened?" said David. The continued to stare upward for a few moments but then David shrugged and they continued on.

The trees were thick and green for most of the afternoon but as they approached the cliffs the plants around them began to exhibit signs of distress. Small trees drooped with coverings of brown; leaves and flowers that had been bright and colorful were now dull with tightly closed petals. Sir Heads-a-lot sniffed at the brown grass. "Something is not right," he said. They heeded his intuition and advanced carefully. Queenie suddenly barked and darted off, so Kira followed and came to a clearing at the base of the cliffs.

In the center of the clearing was a tall tree, which looked quite dead. Its stark branches clawed at the sky. A large hole in the side of the tree showed that it was mostly hollow inside. The cliff face in front of them was a mass of tangled brown vines, thick and impenetrable. The vines completely blocked a narrow opening in the rock wall.

Sir Heads-a-lot reappeared as himself and they all surveyed the area. Aradel walked away, looking for other openings in the rocks. Kira began to hack at the vines. David examined the dead tree. Sir Heads-a-lot glanced nervously at the trees behind them, transformed into an eagle and flapped awkwardly up and out of the clearing to take a look around. He returned moments later, fluttering very un-eagle like to the ground and transformed back into his normal self. "This is the only break in the cliffs for as far as the eye can see. There does appear to be a path beyond the vines if we can get past them. If we have to search for another way in it will take days." He shook his head and together he and David watched Kira attack the vines while they waited for Aradel to return.

"This is impossible," she panted. Every time she cut a vine, two more appeared. Her efforts were only succeeding in making the vines even more impenetrable than before. As soon as she realized the futility of it all, she stopped and sat down with her back to the vines. "We'll have to find another way in."

Aradel appeared looking even more dour than usual. "There doesn't appear to be any other way in."

Sir Heads-a-lot nodded. "I agree. I flew up and looked around, and I didn't see anything but more cliffs and vines."

"Maybe we can climb the vines," said David.

Kira looked at the vines. "No toeholds. We'll never be able to climb it. Sir Heads-a-lot, could you fly up with a rope?"

Sir Heads-a-lot shook his head sadly. "No, I can barely

lift myself off the ground. There's no way I could fly carrying a heavy rope."

"Death is preferable to this existence." This unexpected statement issued from the hole in the dead tree, in a low moan that sounded like the wind.

They all scrambled away from the tree as it spoke again. "The way is closed to you until that which has been denied is revived." The tree fell silent.

David spoke to the tree, "What has been denied?" but there was no reply.

They searched in vain as the sun began to set. David used his wand to pour water on the roots and the vines. It had no effect. Sir Heads-a-lot hoisted David up into the dead tree and he clambered up and searched among the branches for some sign that would help them solve the problem. As the sun set, they were no closer to the answer than when they had started. David built the fire as far from the tree as possible and Aradel, Kira, and Sir Heads-a-lot established guard rotation. They settled into an uneasy sleep. The chrysalis said nothing.

David opened his eyes and stared up at the sky. He could hear the others stirring close by. He slowly rolled over and looked at the dead tree. The rising sun was bathing the clearing with light and warmth. The shadow of the tree crept along the ground and crawled up the rocky cliff. As David stared at the shadow he noticed that one of the branches resembled an arrow and its shadow was pointing to a small outcropping on the rock wall. David was wide-awake now. He hurried over to Sir Heads-a-lot.

"Put me on your shoulders, over by that outcropping," he said while pointing at the shadow. But even then he couldn't reach the outcropping. Sir Heads-a-lot put him down and reached into a pocket. In moments a giraffe stood in front of David and lowered its head to the ground. David climbed on and the head rose until he was high above the clearing and level with the outcropping.

"What do you see?" Kira was staring upward.

David was disappointed. "It's just a rock." He leaned over to examine the outcropping closely and as he did he lost his balance and fell forward. His hands grasped for the outcropping and he grabbed it as the giraffe struggled to catch him. As his weight came down on the rock, it shifted and pivoted out of the wall. With a scream David fell and landed softly on top of what felt like a big bowl of gelatin. He looked down and found himself splayed out on top of Aradel who had cushioned his fall. Sir Heads-a-lot hurried over to David, stuffing the giraffe head back into a pocket.

"I'm sorry. I guess I'm awkward with land animals as well as flying animals."

David struggled up off of Aradel. "It's OK, I'm not hurt. Thanks for saving me, Aradel."

A light mist began falling.

They looked up at the outcropping. The rock had shifted downward and a blue mist was now jetting from a small hole high above their heads. As the mist settled on the tree they watched a miraculous transformation. The bark of the tree changed from dry, dead brown to a vibrant blue-green and leaves burst out of every dead bud, washing the tree in a wave of green. Large fragrant white flowers blossomed over the tree.

"What was lost has been found," said the tree in a strong voice. "The way has been opened." A small round stone appeared in the hollow of the tree and was pushed out as the tree was restored. The hole vanished and the stone fell to the ground.

They watched in amazement as the vines on the wall swelled and blossomed until white flowers covered the rocks and then the vines began to untwist and pull back exposing an opening in the cliff. David turned as the mist continued to fall and watched the dead forest beyond the clearing begin to turn green again. He hurried over to the tree and picked up the stone. As the blue mist hit the stone it grew warm in his hand and then darkened to a black and red polished jewel.

Kira stared at the stone. "A healing stone," she breathed.

David looked quickly at the amulet around his neck and at the green chrysalis occupying the central cage. He smiled. "Well, what are we waiting for?" He put the healing stone in his pocket.

They packed up their camp. Kira whistled for Queenie and they stepped into the opening in the cliff. They found themselves in a narrow crevice and in a completely different environment, that to David resembled a rainforest. The same light mist was falling from the rocks above them. Vines and plants flourished along the rock walls. A large overhang, as well as outcroppings all over the walls, blocked most of the sunlight. Aradel seemed pleased for once.

"We can't be seen too well from the air and the overhang hides most of this path from prying eyes. I'd call that a bit of luck. It's about time we had some good luck for a change. Nothing else has gone right on this trip."

David disagreed. "We've made good progress. Thane hasn't succeeded with any of his attacks and we saved the vortex. We helped Sir Heads-a-lot and Houdin is still with us."

Kira put her arm around him. "Aradel doesn't mean anything by it. He's just a grouchy old mano." She smiled up at the mano, who grimaced and turned away.

They marched down the narrow path. David figured that they would be at the lake by lunchtime, but it was early afternoon before they reached the end of the path. Kira stopped suddenly. David could see that a huge stone door covered with holes as big as his hand blocked their way. The holes formed the shape of a gigantic spool. In the center of the spool was a larger hole. Dim light was shining through all the holes.

"I guess we might as well eat lunch while we try to figure out what to do next," Kira said, as she began unpacking some food. They ate a quick lunch while they contemplated the door. They each took a turn looking through the large hole in the center of the door.

When David had his turn, he had to get Kira to hold him up so he could see. Beyond the door was a long wide cavern. At the far end of the cavern was another door. He could barely see the door but it appeared to have the same spool pattern on it, only the shadows obscured his view.

When Aradel slid up to look David suddenly shouted, "There's a picture on the ground." Aradel had wiped the dirt off of a diagram carved into the stone floor in front of the door. They all crowded around trying to see in the narrow corridor while David swept the remaining dust out of the cracks of the carving. The carving was of a hand next to a circle. Next to that was another hand, and next to that a tiny spool pattern like the one on the door.

"What do you think it means?" Kira asked.

"What if it's a picture of a hand covering one of the holes?" David said.

They tried various combinations of covering the holes in the pattern but nothing happened. Finally Aradel decided to find out what was on the other side of the door. He handed all his weapons to Sir Heads-a-lot and then oozed through the central hole in the door. Once he was on the other side he began to advance into the cavern, but he had moved only a few steps when suddenly a bright light flashed through the cavern and, while they watched in horror, the mano was frozen to the spot.

Kira beat against the stone in a futile attempt to get through to help Aradel. She lifted David up to see and he began squinting at the scene in front of him.

The cavern remained brightly lit and David noticed that the light refracting off of the icy covering of the frozen mano created a magnifying glass effect. He could look through the mano and see the door at the far end of the cavern. It was greatly magnified and now he could see that the spool pattern on the door was a series of X's and O's. The X's must tell us which ones to cover up, he thought.

After a quick count he realized they had a problem. There were 18 X's. We only have six hands. He explained his theory to Kira and Sir Heads-a-lot. A quick change of heads and they were up to twelve if you counted the eight arms of the octopus that was sitting in the dirt where Sir Heads-a-lot had been. David grinned. They made a great team.

He took off his jacket and the four spectrum sacks that he carried. They used the sacks and the jacket in the top holes, which David had to reach from Kira's shoulders. Consulting the pattern frequently, they used Sir Heads-a-lot's tentacles to block the lower holes. David laughed at the sight. It's like a big game of Twister. Sir Heads-a-lot had tentacles going every which way with some crossed over the others and one stretching almost beyond his reach. Kira was standing on the tips of her toes with her arms stretched wide to block 2 holes and her head tilted to cover the central hole. David reached up and placed his hands over the last two holes. Nothing happened!

David waited until his arms were aching and, disappointed, he started to remove his hands when the door swung forward with a grinding sound. Kira toppled over with a yell, and Sir Heads-a-lot was dragged by his tentacles into the cavern. Queenie rushed ahead barking loudly.

David helped remove the tentacles from the door. Sir Heads-a-lot returned to his normal form and helped to retrieve the spectrum sacks and jacket. Kira climbed out of the dust and rushed over to Aradel. She carefully began to chip at the icy covering on the frozen mano with the handle of her machete. The ice was not thick and it splintered, cracked and slid to the floor in big sheets. Aradel stood still for a moment while his eyes blinked rapidly and then he shivered uncontrollably.

"Well, that was unpleasant," he chattered.

Kira got his coat out of his pack and wrapped it around his shoulders. Once they were sure Aradel was OK they stopped to survey the cavern.

They were at one end of a brightly lit cavern. On the left wall, water poured out of a perfectly round hole and cascaded down into a pool. In the center of the room was a raised platform containing an ornate stone bowl. David walked over to the bowl and looked in to find that it was full of round colorful stones with flashes of light visible inside.

He reached for a stone.

"Don't touch them!" Kira yelled as she scrambled to stop his hand.

David turned to look at her but his hand was still moving and grasped one of the stones. As soon as his fingers closed on the stone the lights in the cavern went out and a single point of light appeared near the platform. It brightened like a spotlight until David was forced to shield his eyes. Then it slowly resolved itself into a man in flowing purple robes holding an ornately carved staff. The man stared at David.

David turned sheepishly to Kira, "Oops."

The man spoke, "I am the Doorcliff guardian. Your Magical Wrestle Fight challenge is accepted. Succeed and you and your friends will be allowed to pass. Fail and all the guardians of the lake will refuse your request."

"I didn't challenge you," said David.

"I'm afraid that you did. You touched the wrestle stones, didn't you?" asked the puzzled guardian.

"Yes, but I didn't know that constituted a challenge."

"Nevertheless, the rules are clear. The challenge has been issued and will be answered or you must leave this place."

David stared in dismay at his companions. Kira wasn't sure what to do and turned to Aradel, who threw off his coat and moved to stand protectively in front of Kira and Sir Heads-a-lot.

"Will you accept a substitute for the challenge?" he asked the man.

"No, the challenge goes to the one who touched the stones."

David tried to fight down his fear. "What do I have to do?"

The guardian relaxed and came to stand next to David. He gestured at the stones. "Each of these stones will be endowed with a particular magical ability which can be used against your opponent. They will be scattered throughout this cavern. The effect of each stone is very short and when you grasp the stone the image of its effect will be projected in your mind."

David nodded his head in understanding but the rules were not entirely clear to him. "What is the goal?"

The guardian pointed to the door at the far end of the cavern. "There is a depression in the center of that door. The first one to reach the door and place his hand in the depression will be the winner."

David protested. "You have an unfair advantage. You know what the stones can do. I need time to learn before I can be effective."

The guardian nodded. "I know what the stones can do but I do not know which stones I will encounter as we traverse the cavern. I will tell you what the possible spells are that will be placed on the stones. Will that satisfy you?"

David was still not sure but the guardian did not look like there was much room for compromise. "Yes, that will do." He thought to himself, I'm counting on the fact that I'm smaller and quicker than he is.

The guardian guided David to the door that they had just come through. They both stood at the threshold and stared down the length of the cavern. The only sound was the steady flow of water into the nearby pool.

"You will encounter stones which will create a strong wind to blow your opponent backward; some will physically move an opponent to a random part of the room. That spell may help your opponent if the random movement is forward. Some stones create holes in the floor, which can be used to halt your opponent's progress, and some will create walls that will have the same effect. You may encounter a stone that will bind your opponent's feet to the floor, stopping his forward motion, or you may encounter a bright light that can be used to blind your opponent temporarily."

David looked at his companions who were standing off to the side and looking very nervous. "Can I be injured or killed in this fight?"

"This fight is one of speed and intelligence. The spells are not threatening. Once a stone is used, its power is exhausted."

David was ready. He thought, this could be fun if it weren't so important. I have to get there first or it's all over. We don't have the time to find another way to the lake, and the guardian already said that no other guardian will let us pass if I lose.

The guardian walked to the center of the room, tapped the stones with his staff and returned to stand next to David.

David stared at the stones. "I'm ready."

The guardian tapped his staff on the floor and the bowl full of stones erupted with a clatter onto the floor of the cavern. The guardian strode forward toward a nearby stone and David spied a different stone and dove forward to grab it. The stone, like every other stone, was black with red streaks. As his hand closed on it, his mind saw the wind stone and the stone turned silver. He aimed the stone at the guardian who was bending to pick up his own stone. A gust of wind blew the guardian backward and the stone almost immediately dimmed to black. David dropped it and started looking for the next one as he advanced across the cavern.

The guardian stumbled forward and grabbed a stone and David found that his feet were glued to the floor. The guardian rushed forward. As suddenly as David had been stopped, his feet were freed and he rushed to grab the next stone. It was a wall stone. He aimed it in front of the guardian and a rock wall rose up out of the floor in front of the guardian. The guardian changed direction and headed for a nearby stone.

David looked and saw two stones close together. He changed course to get the stones but as he did, a hole opened in the floor in front of him. The guardian stood nearby grinning, as he dropped the stone he had in his hand. The floor turned solid again and David grabbed for the two stones. A light stone and a random movement stone. David pocketed the random movement stone and used the light stone. The guardian, even though he wasn't looking at David, was affected and was forced to wait until his vision cleared.

For the next ten minutes the battle went back and forth. David got within a couple of feet of the door when he suddenly found himself standing next to the guardian after a random movement stone was used on him. The guardian reached triumphantly for the door but David picked up another wind stone and was able to advance again while the guardian picked himself up off the floor and searched for another stone. David was forced to use his reserve random movement stone and he was glad to see that the guardian ended up halfway down the cavern. The next stone David recovered was a wind stone, and because he was much closer to the door and he was getting tired he decided to hold onto the stone.

The guardian continued to move up the cavern and stop David with various stones but the stones were becoming few and far between. David used the moments between attacks to get closer and closer to the door but the guardian was right behind him. Now the guardian was next to him and at that moment David pulled out the wind stone, turned to face the center of the room, and with a wide grin he used the wind stone on himself. The gust of wind hit him, picked him up and threw him backward. He ran into the door, spun, and placed his hand in the depression even as he felt the guardian's hand slam down on top of his.

"Well played," said the guardian.

"Better luck next time," said David with a happy laugh. There was the sound of light clapping coming from the pool and David turned to see Fred and Michelle lounging in the pool. Fred was wearing sunglasses and Michelle was munching popcorn.

"Bravo, what a show," enthused Michelle.

"Let's see that again," cheered Fred.

Kira, Sir Heads-a-lot, and Aradel all rushed forward and crowded around David congratulating him. Queenie sensed the excitement and joined in, her tail whipping back and forth.

David was laughing and enjoying the praise from his friends when suddenly a burst of color flashed in front of his eyes. He looked up to see a beautiful orange and black butterfly fluttering in the air above him. Smiling, he reached for his wand, performed the mindmeld, and welcomed Houdin back into their midst.

"What did I miss?" said the wizard.

"We have lots to tell you. I'm glad you're back though. I missed you."

The wizard paused, "I missed you too."

The guardian was now grinning and wiping sweat from his face. "An interesting strategy. Using a stone, not against your opponent but against yourself to improve your position. Commendable." He rapped on the door with his staff. "The way is open."

The door emitted a grinding sound and slowly pivoted to reveal a small room beyond: a room that appeared to have no exit. The guardian waved them forward. "Welcome to Doorcliff."

11 ✱ DOORCLIFF

They grabbed their supplies and went through the now open door into the small room. David turned to the guardian to ask about the room, but the guardian just smiled and stepped away from the door as it swung closed, plunging the small room into darkness. But it wasn't quite dark, for as David's eyes adjusted he could see that a soft glow was coming from all four sides of the room. As he looked at the glowing walls it became apparent that what they were really looking at was a room full of doors. There was one door on each wall including the door that they had just come through.

Kira went to the door on the left and reached out with her hand to touch it. The door opened to reveal swirling red mist, then swung shut again. Aradel shrugged and touched the center door, which swung open to reveal purple mist and when Sir Heads-a-lot touched the door on the right it revealed yellow mist.

"Which one do we choose?" asked Kira. She prodded the wall again and tried to look through the red mist but it was too thick to see anything beyond the door. David examined the doors, which were entirely smooth. He touched Kira's door, which opened again, but this time the mist was orange!

Now they all moved from door to door. Each time they switched doors, the color of the mist behind the door changed.

If a person opened the same door a second time in a row, the color stayed the same. As they continued experimenting, the left hand door showed yellow, green, blue, midnight blue and purple. The center door went from purple to red, then orange, white, green, sky blue, and midnight blue. The door on the right was green, pink, midnight blue, purple, red, orange, and yellow.

Sir Heads-a-lot put on an owl head and tried to see beyond the mist but failed. Aradel tossed small pebbles into the mist but all they heard was the clatter of the stones falling on the floor beyond the doors. They even tried the door back into the cavern, but it wouldn't open.

"Obviously, we are meant to continue on. We must choose a path," Houdin said.

They ran through the colors again for each door but they still couldn't see how to choose. Queenie tried to go through a door but Kira held her back while they tried to decide.

"Let's just pick one," said an impatient Kira, and Aradel agreed. David couldn't come up with anything better so they decided to try the right hand door, but just as they opened it and started to step through David yelled, "Stop, I think that's the wrong door!"

Kira paused with her foot on the threshold and turned inquiringly back to look at David. "Why?"

David was thinking furiously. He turned to the door on the left. "This one. I'm sure of it."

Aradel was impatient to try anything, so he slid over to the door. "Fine, one's as good as the other." He touched the door, it slid open and he slid forward into the red mist and disappeared. Kira and Queenie hurried after him, followed by David and Houdin and finally Sir Heads-a-lot. As Sir Heads-a-lot cleared the threshold the door swung shut behind them and wouldn't open again.

"Why this door?" growled Aradel as they began to feel their way through the mist which was now orange.

"Roy G. Biv" said David.

"Huh?" The mist turned yellow.

"The colors of the rainbow are red, orange, yellow, green, blue, indigo, and violet. This was the only door that had all the right colors. The other doors had white and pink so I thought this was the best choice."

Houdin was impressed. "Brilliant. A good choice. Let's hope it's the right one."

Aradel suddenly stopped and they all ploughed into him because they couldn't see him through the mist. As they got up, wiping the slime from their clothes, they could see why Aradel had stopped. They were at another door.

Kira touched it and it swung open to reveal stone steps wreathed in white mist. They stepped through and knew immediately that they were outside. They could feel the sun's warmth hidden behind a curtain of mist and were refreshed by the light breeze that caressed their faces. They began to climb through the mist. Houdin tried to flutter above the mist but with water settling on his wings he had to content himself with sitting on David's shoulder and listening to David as he told all the things that had happened since they were in the tunnel to FarPass.

"You've done better than I could have dreamed," said Houdin. David blushed at the praise but he felt really happy. He had missed talking to Houdin and they seemed to be on the right path that would take them to Thane. They still had time.

They climbed through the mist for several hours and as they climbed the sound of rushing water began to grow. They finally reached the top where they found their way blocked by a heavy covering of vines covered with sharp thorns. Kira began to cut away the vines and this time they stayed cut and fell to the ground in bunches, but it was slow going and David was impatient to see what was on the other side. While Kira worked, he looked and found an opening through the vines close to the ground and began crawling through. He made himself as small as possible but even then he could feel the vines poking him and snagging on his clothes and the spectrum sacks. But he was able to get through and soon enough Kira had hacked a passage for the rest of them.

They stepped out of the mist into a dusky sun that was just beginning to set. A red door stood in front of them, but amazingly the door didn't lead anywhere. There were no walls—just a door. On either side of the door they could see all of Lake Istep visible below them. To their left a magnificent waterfall cascaded over the cliff with a thundering sound. As they gathered on the edge to survey their surroundings, Fred and Michelle came floating by on a piece of driftwood. They waved at everyone and then noticed the butterfly perched on David's shoulder, his wings drying in the sun. "Nice outfit, Houdin!" They laughed and then, as their piece of wood was swept over the waterfall, they squealed, "Aiiiiiiiiiiieeeeeeeeeeeeeeee!" They disappeared over the edge on their own personal log flume ride.

David looked over the cliff and he could see almost the entire lake. A big dark shape was visible under the water gliding back and forth around small stepping-stones that stretched from the shoreline toward the center of the lake, where they could see a large castle. Several of the turrets were crumbling but one turret still stood tall and proud in the fading light. As they pondered what to do, they watched the castle and were rewarded by the sight of a man coming out onto the lone parapet at the top of the turret. They couldn't see his features from this distance but they did see him raise his arms to the sky and blazing streams of spectrum began climbing into the sky. They watched as the spectrum caught the upper air stream and swirled away to vanish into the growing darkness.

"It's got to be Thane," said Houdin.

While the others watched the castle Sir Heads-a-lot opened the red door, which swung out over the cliff, and peered through it, looking down at the lake and the distant shoreline. Queenie sat nearby, tongue lolling out of her mouth.

Two small animals darted out of the mist and ran through the door. Queenie barked and jumped after them as Kira lunged for her shouting, "No!" But she was too late. Queenie leaped through the open door . . . and vanished!

David stared at the empty air beyond the door. Queenie

hadn't fallen. One minute she was there and the next minute she was gone, along with the two little animals that had gone through so fast that David wasn't even sure he had seen them at all.

Kira was staring down the cliff and crying. "She's gone. I can't believe she would do that. She's usually so smart." Her sobbing broke off into confused sniffles. "It looks like you might have been wrong David. This path leads nowhere. We'll have to go back and try again with a different door."

Sir Heads-a-lot was leaning far out over the cliff now and staring down at the ground far below them. "Do you hear that?" They all came over and bent down to listen. David could hear a faint barking.

"She's still alive!" cried Kira.

Aradel went over to look at the door. "Where is she? What happened when she went through the door?" He grabbed the side of the doorway and stretched his hand out as far as he could and everyone gasped as his arm disappeared. He pulled his arm back and stared at it. "It didn't feel any different yet we couldn't see it."

Queenie's barking grew louder as they tried to decide what to do.

David was staring over the cliff. "Well, it seems like Queenie is OK. We should try it ourselves." Kira looked apprehensive but hearing Queenie's barking seemed to strengthen her resolve.

While the others were trying to convince themselves that David might be right, he decided to test his theory. He began tossing pebbles through the door. Every single one simply vanished as it went through the plane of the door. David was convinced. He stood up, looked at the others and stepped through the door, seemingly placing his feet in the empty air at the edge of the cliff . . . and vanished!

The others stared over the cliff. Queenie stopped barking and David's voice came wafting up from below. "I'm OK. Come on down." The others looked at each other and then Kira shrugged and marched through the open door. The others quickly followed and in moments the cliff was empty except for the red door swinging in the breeze and the mist swirling over the stairway.

David was astounded and excited at the same time. He had stepped through the door and where there should have been air, he felt sand. As he went through the door the sight of the lake and castle below him had vanished and reappeared instantly but now the perspective was from the ground. It was very disorienting. Now he was looking at the castle across the lake and staring up at Thane standing on the parapet of the turret. He turned to look back and found a green doorway built into the side of the cliff. Beyond the doorway was rock and as he looked, Kira stepped out of the rock as if it wasn't even there, followed by Houdin, Sir Heads-a-lot and Aradel.

"Now that's the way to travel," said Sir Heads-a-lot looking up at the cliff and trying to see the red door, but the cliff was wreathed in darkness and mist and he couldn't see where the door was. Aradel had moved to the edge of the lake and was looking out at the distant castle and the stepping-stones that led across the lake. Kira was rolling around with Queenie and laughing.

"I thought I'd lost you. Don't you dare jump through any more magical doors." Queenie happily slobbered over anyone who came close to her.

Houdin fluttered over to David. "Don't take foolish chances like that," he scolded. "I don't want to have to keep my promise to notify your parents."

"But I had a theory," David protested. "And it turned out to be right!"

"Yes, but if you'd told me your theory, I could have flown out and tested it more safely!" Houdin exclaimed.

David looked down. "Sorry."

Aradel was surveying the sky, which was darkening as the sun went down, and he now moved them back from the edge of the lake toward the shadows of the cliff. "We need to try and keep Thane from knowing how close we are."

Kira pointed near the doorway. "Well there's another dead mouse, so we seem to be having some luck."

David stared at the mouse. "How do you know Thane controlled that mouse?"

Kira chuckled. "I don't, but if he did it's never going to be able to tell Thane we're here." She stared at the others. "We need to camp here tonight, but no fire."

They ate a light dinner of bread and fruit and watched a beautiful sunset on the lake. The amount of spectrum in the clouds, illuminated by the rays of dying light created a spectacle of color that made everybody's heart a little lighter, but as the shadows deepened and the castle descended into darkness, the exhaustion and uneasiness they all felt returned.

David now had the time to remove the healing stone from his pocket and place it back in the cage of the amulet, which still contained the discarded chrysalis. David removed the chrysalis and placed it carefully in his pocket. Houdin waited, and when David was done he spoke up.

"We need to practice a spell to use against Thane. I think that a binding spell will be our quickest and best chance. It's complex enough that Thane won't expect it but not too difficult for you to master. You will need plenty of earth and air spectrum for this one. Look up the Wind Binding spell."

David took out the spell books, and by consulting the books and working with Houdin he was soon able to use the binding spell pretty well. Sir Heads-a-lot allowed David to practice on him. Each spell created a whirlwind, which enveloped Sir Heads-a-lot and then tightened and spun faster until he found he couldn't lift his arms. David practiced far into the night and by the time he was finished, he could almost accomplish the spell without thinking.

By this time he was so tired that he had to stop, and as soon as he crawled into his sleeping bag he was asleep. Houdin stayed up all night watching the lights of the castle and anticipating the coming morning.

In the morning, Houdin fluttered away to scout ahead over the lake. He was gone for quite some time and they had a cold breakfast while they waited for his return. Soon after they finished, the now colorful wizard fluttered back to them.

"There's a cobralan in the lake!"

"What's a cobralan?" David asked Kira.

Kira started. "Where?"

"Houdin says there is one in the lake."

Kira stared out at the lake. "The cobralan is a very rare animal in Remin. I've never seen one alive. We found their bones all the time and just recently a dead one washed up on the shores of a lake east of Remin. If that dark shape that we saw from the cliff is a cobralan, and it's helping to guard the castle, then we're going to have to stay out of the lake."

"It is a cobralan," hissed Houdin. "It's a large fish with multiple pairs of wing-like fins and an enormous sail fin on its back," he explained to David. "It's very dangerous. It has an enormous round mouth and long whisker-like appendages on its head. Altogether, it's as big as a house."

David raised one eyebrow, but decided not to contradict Houdin.

Houdin, noticing David's polite disbelief, said, "Well, at least a small house."

Standing in the shadows of the cliff they stared across the lake at the castle, now bathed in early morning light. The step stones jutted out of the calm lake. Kira shouldered her pack and strode across the beach, splashing through the water to reach the first stone. Standing knee-deep in the lake, she lifted her foot and stepped up onto the stone.

David watched as she leaped from stone to stone and slowly moved out onto the lake. He gasped when the next stone she jumped onto sank under her as she stepped on it. "Kira, the cobralan!"

The water in the center of the lake churned. A large sail-fin jutted out of the water and moved toward her. She swam back and scrambled onto the last solid stone. The stone that had sunk now reappeared. Kira attempted the stone again but again it sank. She then tried to jump over it to the next stone but that stone also sank. Each attempt brought the cobralan closer to investigate the commotion in the water. She climbed out the last time and, dripping, made her way back to the beach, joining her companions in the shadows again.

Squeezing water from the hem of her tunic, she grimaced. "Now what do we do?"

"Let me try," pleaded David. "I'm the lightest one here, except for Queenie. Maybe the stones are sensitive to weight."

Houdin protested, "No! It's too dangerous."

"Even if you're right, how will the rest of us get through?" said Aradel.

Sir Heads-a-lot stepped up. "Let him try it," he argued. "He's already taken plenty of chances and proved himself capable. If David can get across, maybe he can find a way to help us from the other side." Sir Heads-a-lot and David argued with the others until, worn down and without any other hope, they gave in and decided to let David make the attempt.

David removed his jacket and belt and waded out to the first stone. The water was up to his chest as he clambered onto the first stone. From there he made the leaps out to the last solid stone and stared at the problem stone as the fin of the cobralan knifed through the water in front of him. Finally he screwed up his courage and made the leap. The stone started to sink as he landed on it but stabilized and remained upright as David readied himself for the next leap. He jumped to the next stone and as he did the problem stone clicked loudly and rose a few more inches out of the water.

Kira, Aradel and Sir Heads-a-lot had seen his success with the sinking rock so they moved out to catch up with him. Soon they were spread out across the lake with Kira on the last solid stone, Sir Heads-a-lot on the next stone back and Aradel on the rock behind that. Queenie watched intently from the beach. David waited, three stones in front of Kira. When she was ready, Kira leaped to the stone and found that it was solid again, but when she jumped for the next stone it sank again and she was forced to clamber back once more.

"Now what?" she called out to David. He studied the stones and made the leap to the next one. The rock in front of Kira clicked and rose up. Kira leaped and it stayed underneath her feet. In this way, they made their way across the lake with David staying ahead of the group and triggering the stones so they wouldn't sink.

But as they got closer and closer to the castle the stones started to get farther apart and David had more trouble making the leaps. His last two leaps missed and he ended up in the water clambering onto the next stone. On the last leap the cobralan flashed by under his feet as he leaped and in a panic he climbed onto the next stone. He stared at the next stone, which was way beyond any jump he could make. He would have to swim to get to it. It was the last stone. Beyond it was a large body of water and then the shores of Salvar. He wasn't sure how they were going to get to the actual island.

"I have to swim for the next one," he called back to Kira.

"No!" Aradel yelled out. "It's too dangerous. You can't risk it; the cobralan is too close."

"Well what are we going to do?"

Aradel sighed. "When I tell you I'm ready, I want you to run for it."

David watched as Aradel glanced at the cobralan fin and then quickly lowered himself silently into the water. He jetted through the water until he was even with the rock that David was standing on, and then he floated on his back with his head pointing at the next rock. As David watched, his body began to elongate and stretch, oozing across the water and forming a bridge between the two rocks. The dark shape of the cobralan flashed by underneath the mano, who stopped stretching and tried to remain perfectly still. The mano stretched again as the cobralan turned and was soon near the next rock.

"Now," Aradel whispered urgently.

David knew they were in a dangerous spot so he immediately ran forward. It felt like he was running in quicksand. Aradel's body was soft and squishy as he made his way across the mano bridge. In moments he was clambering onto the next rock. Time seemed to stand still as the familiar click sounded and the rock in front of Kira rose up. Then there was another click and the rock David was standing on rose up, and a whole line of rocks rose out of the water in front of him making an easy path to the island. David smiled and turned to help Aradel who was shrinking back to his normal form, but the smile turned to horror as the cobralan flashed by upside down with a gaping mouth aiming for Aradel.

"Hurry, Aradel, it's coming."

Aradel rolled over and grabbed at the stone David was standing on. David stepped onto the next stone and watched as Aradel started to climb out, but at that moment the water behind Aradel erupted and the cobralan rose up and pounced on the mano, knocking him off the rock and carrying him away. David saw the gaping mouth swoop onto the struggling mano, who disappeared. The water frothed and then grew calm again.

Houdin fluttered above the water where Aradel had disappeared. Kira finished the leaps and arrived next to David with tears on her face. She stared at the spot where the cobralan had disappeared. As Sir Heads-a-lot arrived, David moved down another stone. Queenie now barked and Kira signaled her to come. The wolfat ran excitedly to the water and clambered onto the first stone and then leapfrogged across the lake to join the rest of the group. They all clambered across the stone path and reached the island of Salvar.

Kira stared out at the water. "I can't believe he's gone," she said glumly. The fin of the cobralan reappeared momentarily and then its tail convulsively slapped the water and vanished.

They all bowed their heads in silent grief, and as they did so, they heard a loud click. David looked up quickly, and as he did so, he caught a gray streak of movement out of the corner of his eye. But he immediately forgot it when he saw that the nearest stones were sinking back into the water. "I guess we'll have to find another way back," he said glumly. "That is, if we make it back."

Kira handed David his jacket and rope belt. Then they turned to stare at the castle that loomed over their heads.

12 ✶ SALVAR CASTLE

They moved quickly across the beach but as they neared the castle wall Kira suddenly stopped and stared down at her feet. "Go back!" Kira said desperately, but it was too late. They were standing in quicksand! Kira's boots were already covered and David had sunk in to his knees. Sir Heads-a-lot was caught as well. Queenie barked frantically from the edge of the quicksand.

"Don't move!" cried David. "The more you move the faster you sink."

Kira was staring upward at the castle and noticed a low stone crenellated walkway, which encircled the castle. Kira took the rope on her belt, made a loop and began trying to lasso one of the merlons on the wall.

"Hurry, Kira!" David said with an edge of panic in his voice. Kira turned and saw that David had sunk to his waist.

"I'm hurrying as fast as I can," she gasped. But her attempts failed again and again and her panting grew more ragged as she began to tire.

The quicksand crept up to David's chest and he could hear his rapid heartbeat thudding in his ears. And we came so far, he thought in despair.

Houdin fluttered in front of him. "Get your wand, quickly!"

David fumbled to get his wand out and sank to his armpits. He raised the wand over his head.

"Concentrate on the lasso. You want to imagine that you can control the lasso using the Windtunia spell. Try picturing a swirl of wind that moves the lasso where you want it. Hurry!"

Kira was slumped in the quicksand, the lasso lying next to her. David concentrated as hard as he could.

"Windtunia!"

A burst of silver spectrum climbed out of his wand. He pointed his wand at the lasso and the spectrum exploded into a gust of wind, which lifted the lasso and held it hovering in the air next to Kira. She lifted her head in astonishment. David's eyes widened but he kept staring at the hovering rope. He lifted it higher and higher, using the wand to guide it. He poured all of his energy into pushing the lasso toward the wall. The stream of spectrum poured from his wand. The lasso inched forward until it hovered over the wall, and then David lowered the loop over the merlon. He slumped in complete exhaustion.

Even though he had tried to keep his movements small, they had caused him to slip further into the quicksand. He had to hold his arms up to keep them free. He couldn't do anything more.

But Kira, energized by the lifeline that David had procured for them, tightened the rope and pulled herself free of the quicksand, extending her foot so that David could grab it. Hand over hand she pulled herself up until they were both free of the clinging mud. David grabbed for Kira's walking stick as she pulled them up to the wall and they were able to swing over to the solid ground at the base of the wall. Queenie made a running jump over the quicksand to join Kira and David. Sir Heads-a-lot, who was much taller than the rest, was only up to his chest when Kira got the rope to him and soon the entire group was safe at the foot of the castle. They checked their supplies and found that their only loss was a bag of fruit.

Kira tried to wipe some of the muck off of her clothes. "Well it can't get much worse than that, can it?" she grinned.

David smiled and raised his wand and produced a stream of water that they all used to rinse off some of the mud. Kira examined the rope. "I guess we've killed two birds with one stone. We were looking for a way into the castle and we now have a rope neatly tied to the walkway surrounding the castle. So up we go!" She used the rope to pull herself up the side of the castle to the walkway. Sir Heads-a-lot helped tie David to the rope and Kira pulled him up. Next she pulled up Queenie, who whined when she was lifted off the ground, but calmed when she heard Kira's voice soothing her. Sir Heads-a-lot pulled himself up with Kira's help. He tumbled over the wall, spilling some his heads, and as they hurried to pick up the heads a shuffling sound suddenly came from behind them.

"Someone's coming," whispered Kira urgently.

Houdin fluttered upward. "It's a mano guard!"

Queenie began growling, but Kira shushed her and they began running down the walkway. Kira spotted an iron door and tried to open it. "I guess it would be too much to expect to have an unlocked entrance," she said. But then she turned to Sir Heads-a-lot. "I have an idea." They gathered around her as she told them her plan. "First we'll pretend that we're trying to open this door."

Moments later the guard appeared behind them. "Stop where you are," said the guard, leveling a spear at them. A crossbow hung from his chain mail vest.

"We give up," said David as he stepped forward with his hands up. Kira and Sir Heads-a-lot tried to step between David and the guard.

The guard herded them together with his spear and then reached around and opened the iron door with a large set of keys. "It's the dungeons for all of you until Thane has time to deal with you."

The guard prodded them into the castle, which was brightly lit with flaming torches.

Houdin fluttered discreetly behind them muttering to himself. "This is a bad plan. If this fails we will be in real trouble."

163

With pokes from his spear and occasional gruff commands, the guard guided them deep into the castle. David could see that much of the interior was in ruins. Large stones and rubble filled most of the rooms and daylight filtered in through gaping holes in the outer walls and ceilings.

When they reached the dungeons, the mano pushed a small lever next to a massive stone door, which swung open to reveal a corridor lined with doors. They marched down the corridor until the mano stopped them before another large iron door, which he unlocked with his keys. The door was perforated with small holes for air and a small sliding panel, which opened to provide food for the prisoners. The guard shoved Kira into the cell. "All of you, inside now."

As Kira stepped through the door, David stopped and bent down. "Wait, my sandal strap came undone."

The mano guard stopped and turned to watch as David fastened the strap on his sandal. At that moment an eight-foot boa constrictor rose up from the spot where Sir Heads-a-lot had been standing. All of the mano's eyes turned a surprised look at the snake, and his spear clattered to the ground. The snake slithered over and coiled around the guard immobilizing him. Kira picked up the spear and took the crossbow. The mano guard tried to slip out of the coils but the snake tightened its grip until the mano stopped struggling.

They pushed the mano inside the cell and locked the door with the keys. David watched as Sir Heads-a-lot transformed back to his normal form and stood there grinning.

"An excellent plan, Kira."

"Manos have never seen someone like you so they don't know what to expect, and this one didn't expect an eight foot snake," said Kira with a chuckle.

"I still don't understand how a snake could immobilize a mano," said David. "Back at the dome, I saw Aradel stick a sword through himself to carry it. Why didn't the snake just go right through the jelly?"

"Mano in their normal state are almost solid," Kira

answered. "That's what allows them to have a form and walk around. But they can change their consistency to a near liquid jelly when it is convenient. That's how Aradel was able to put a sword through himself without injury. But the mano guard was startled and didn't have time to make the change. When they are in their near-solid form, they can be immobilized, hurt, or even killed. Now, we should get out of here quickly. The cell won't hold that mano guard for long."

Houdin was ecstatic. "We just need to get to the tower. I watched the castle last night and the only lights that were burning all night were in the tower rooms, so Thane must be there."

They ran down the corridor to the dungeon entrance but found the massive stone door closed and locked. Kira examined the door and tried to lever it open with the end of her machete but couldn't even get the blade into the cracks at the edges.

"How do the mano get out of here? There's no locking mechanism on this side of the door. The only lever is on the other side." They continued to examine the door. Finally, they found a small stone that could be removed to reveal a round hole. David tried in vain to get his hand through the hole but it was too small.

"The mano must change their arm to near-liquid form and ooze it through this hole to trigger the lever," said Sir Heads-a-lot thoughtfully. They spent the next couple of minutes trying every item they had with them, including octopus tentacles and deer antlers courtesy of Sir Heads-a-lot, but none could trigger the door.

They began searching up and down the corridor and finally found a small area of an upper wall with a small hole in it. Houdin fluttered into the hole and returned moments later. "It's a tight fit but it leads to a corridor near the dungeon entrance." Sir Heads-a-lot hoisted David up to take a look.

"I think I can fit through here," said David. He stripped off his jacket and belt and handed them to Kira and then pulled his wand out and squeezed it, forcing it to give off a soft glow. He stuck the wand in the hole, pulled himself in, and began inching through the tiny opening. The tunnel through the stone was small and in some places he had to exhale deeply in order to force himself through. The dust he kicked up made him cough and his fear began to grow as the tunnel got smaller and more claustrophobic, but just when he was ready to give up and try to inch his way back out, the hole widened and he scrambled through, dropping into a rubble-filled corridor. He ran down the hall, found the dungeon entrance and triggered the door, which swung open to reveal his friends. Kira handed him his jacket and his belt and together they started off to find the tower.

Kira led them upward, moving stealthily toward the center of the castle where the tower was situated. Several times, they heard guards shuffling and were forced to detour or hide, waiting for the danger to pass them. Houdin fluttered ahead, helping to scout their position and guiding them through a maze of corridors and rubble-strewn rooms. David noticed that several of the rooms had dreamweaving murals, which were cracked and peeling. It must have been a beautiful castle, he thought sadly.

Kira halted and gestured for silence. They peered into the next room. It was a large room with a central winding staircase. Two mano guards were patrolling the room.

"Thane must be exerting some kind of control over these mano," said Houdin. "These must be some of the mano who came to try to stop Thane. It's not an easy thing to enslave another person but it's possible."

They watched quietly for several minutes trying to formulate a plan to get past the guards.

"There are only two of them. We can take them with a frontal assault," said Kira.

"Yes, but we've already lost Aradel, we can't afford to risk any more losses," said Sir Heads-a-lot.

"Here's your chance to practice the binding spell," said Houdin.

They decided that David would attempt to ensnare one guard while Sir Heads-a-lot, Kira, and Queenie handled the other one. They waited until one of the guards came close to their position and started their attack.

David aimed his wand, concentrated, and said quietly, "Windtunia." The spell was wildly successful as the spectrum created a whirlwind, which captured the surprised guard and left him helpless.

Queenie ran toward the other guard with Kira and Sir Heads-a-lot close behind. Queenie leaped on the guard, knocking him to the floor. Kira and Sir Heads-a-lot pounced on the struggling guard knocking away his weapons and rolling around as he shouted for help.

David kept the binding spell going as he headed for the stairs. He reached the stairs and watched the continuing struggle with the other mano guard. Kira finally got her hand over the mano's nose and after struggling for air, the flailing mano lapsed into unconsciousness. Queenie joined David and Houdin on the stairs as Kira and Sir Heads-a-lot arrived.

"We have to hurry. His shouting probably warned the whole castle," panted Kira, and as if in answer to her statement loud shufflings and shouts could be heard coming from the rooms beyond the stairs.

They ran up the stairs and as they reached the second landing, a group of mano rushed into the room below them armed with various weapons. They stared upward at the intruders and started for the stairs. Queenie stood at the top of the stairs growling and slobbering with her fur standing on end. A few spears clattered against the upper railing but none of them reached Queenie or the fleeing comrades.

Houdin fluttered through a damaged wall and returned to direct them to a massive wooden door set in a curved wall at the end of the corridor. They opened the door, which revealed the tower stairway. Kira called Queenie to her. They all crowded onto the stairs, pulled the door closed behind them, and barred it with large wooden timbers which Kira and Sir Heads-a-lot struggled to put in place. Just as the timbers slipped into place, the mano began pounding on the other side.

Kira, Sir Heads-a-lot, Queenie, and David crept up the

stairs and reached a small landing, where they were blocked by a double set of wooden doors. Kira left Queenie at the top of the landing with instructions to warn them if the mano succeeded in getting past the door. The wolfat sat staring down the shadowed stairwell.

Kira and Sir Heads-a-lot tried to open the double doors but they were locked. The wooden doors had two large hinges that Kira began working on with her machete. She levered the pins out of one of the hinges and together she and Sir Heads-a-lot pulled the door open wide enough that they could squeeze through. Houdin fluttered in ahead of them. When he returned, the excitement he felt was evident even to Kira and Sir Heads-a-lot, who couldn't hear his words to David.

"This is it!"

13 ✳ THE DARKEST NIGHT

They entered the room under the shadow of broken columns and large stone fragments. An eerie glow shone ahead of them. Kira and Sir Heads-a-lot took up positions on either side of David and together they crept forward towards the light.

The three of them crouched behind a broken column and looked into the room. A simple table and chair sat among the ruins. An ornate full-length mirror hung on one wall near several tattered curtains. A broken mosaic depicting the Imaginator occupied another wall. Stone basins hung on each wall with a trickle of water flowing out of gargoyle heads mounted over each basin.

A tall figure in a dark gray robe stood with his back to them. Thane. His head was hooded and he was looking down at a large glass dome, which was so bright that David's eyes hurt just to look at it. The dome dominated the room. It was almost as tall as the man. Several sacks overflowing with spectrum sat on the floor near the man.

They were much closer than they had been at the vortex and David shuddered. The group had achieved their goal, with the loss of Aradel as the only low point. They had found Thane but now they had to confront and defeat him. Looking at the massive arms on the tall man, David began to doubt that they would be successful.

Thane was muttering to himself. David strained to make out the words. "What's he saying?" he whispered.

Sir Heads-A-Lot fumbled with his vest and then switched heads, removing his normal head, which shrunk to the size of a button, and replacing it with a head he had just removed from his pocket. David continued to be fascinated by the change. The new head expanded until Sir Heads-a-lot crouched there with an elephant head on his shoulders. Sir Heads-a-lot realized that bringing an elephant into the room would not help them maintain their secrecy so he allowed only a partial transformation. The enormous ears flapped forward zeroing in on the muttering coming from across the room. After listening for a moment, the elephant whispered, "He doesn't know we're here. For some reason he thinks we are delayed at Doorcliff."

Houdin fluttered forward and circled high above the dome. He returned quickly. "It's a fully functioning Imaginator, just as we expected. I don't know how he did it. We may not be able to stop him."

Kira drew out her knife, knelt down and quickly scratched in the dirt as they all watched. "David, you wait here while I circle to the left. When I am in position, I will distract Thane and Sir Heads-a-lot can attempt to disarm him. Without his wand, Thane will be much more vulnerable."

Sir Heads-a-lot nodded, removed his elephant head and replaced it, undergoing a full transformation to a fierce bald eagle. The hands were now sharp grasping talons.

Kira continued, "When Thane is disarmed…" and now she turned to David, "it will be up to you. Use the binding spell. You will have to move into the room to cast the spell, as you need Thane in full view. You will have to confront him but as soon as he sees you, cast the spell. Once he is subdued we can attempt to force him to reverse the curse and free Houdin." David swallowed and nodded.

Unseen by anyone, a mouse watched them from the shadows. Its red eyes glittered malevolently. When it had heard enough, it turned and started to scurry away. Just then, a gray shape dropped from the wall above, stopping the mouse in its tracks.

Kira gave one more look around and then slipped off to the left. Sir Heads-a-lot rose into the air and settled on one of the torches lighting the room. Now David was alone with his thoughts. It had all come down to this. He was scared. He grasped his wand, checked it and saw that it was low on spectrum. He reached down to his belt for the earth spectrum but found to his horror that the bag was empty! He checked the bag and found a small tear in it. His eyes filled with tears. "All I have left is fire and air spectrum! I can't accomplish the binding spell. I must have snagged it on the thorns at the top of the cliff and then I wasted too much spectrum practicing." Frantically he tried to get Sir Heads-a-lot's attention but the eagle was concentrating on Thane. David began to move to his left to try and stop Kira but he was too late. A movement on his left told him that the final battle had begun.

Kira appeared, running across the room and attempting a flying tackle of the distracted weaver. Thane heard the crunch of gravel as she started her run and turned to face her. As Kira realized her plan had failed, she skidded to a halt and drew her sword. Her voice rang out, "I will not allow you to destroy Remin!"

Thane laughed and faced her. He held an ornate wooden wand topped by a weaving spool.

"I don't know how you did it." Thane's voice was low and filled with hate. "How did you get in here without my spies seeing you?" he said. "No matter, your companions can come out now." He turned and surveyed the room.

Sir Heads-a-lot swooped down on Thane, intent on removing the wand from his grasp. Thane muttered a spell under his breath and silver spectrum swirled forward in a blast of wind with the force of a hurricane, which hit the eagle and sent it cartwheeling through the air until it smashed into a stone column. The eagle's head came off; Sir Heads-a-lot reappeared and crumpled headless to the ground. As the body hit the floor, hundreds of button-size heads scattered across the room.

David involuntarily cried out and stood up, forgetting the danger. His friend was dead! His eyes filled with tears. Thane stepped forward and snarled, "Impossible. My spies would have warned me. You are a surprise, young one, but you are no match for me. I do not know what magic allowed you to travel here undetected but..." He suddenly stopped.

Out of the shadows a gray striped cat appeared, carrying a dead mouse in its mouth. With a flick of its tail, it dropped the mouse at Thane's feet and walked over to stand beside David. From the other side of the room, a white cat with gray patches brought another mouse to drop at Thane's feet, then went to stand beside David. David's fear disappeared. He laughed. He then whispered to the cats, "Cutie, Spud. Thank you. He is unprepared. We still have a chance."

Houdin fluttered forward and when Thane noticed the colorful butterfly, anger and hatred suddenly disappeared from his face to be replaced by delight. He looked like a totally different person. He laughed and pointed at the fluttering insect. "Ah, Houdin, my old friend, you don't look yourself today. You've lost weight." He continued to chortle, "I am truly amazed that you have made it this far, but it will not help you. Your weakness has always been your choice of companions. They are weak and untrained to deal with someone as powerful as I have become." He glanced with disdain at what was left of Sir Heads-a-lot. "Soon, the curse will take you again and I will still be here, growing in power."

Houdin flew back to where David was standing. "Don't listen to him. He wants you to be afraid."

David muttered under his breath, "He's doing a really good job." He looked up to face Thane, but Thane had dismissed him as unimportant.

Thane turned to face Kira who had been inching toward him in an attempt to get close enough to fight him. The delight he had shown at Houdin's plight was once again replaced by arrogance. The sword in Kira's hands glowed red-hot as Thane shot fire spectrum at the weapon.

Kira dropped the sword, dove sideways, drew her knife, and threw it at Thane's hands. The knife sliced through the billowing sleeve of Thane's robe, cutting into his arm. Blood appeared on the sleeve as the knife clattered to the ground.

At that moment Aradel rose up from behind the dome. David was so surprised to see the mano that he almost dropped his wand, but he had been clutching it so hard that even if he tried, his clenched fingers wouldn't let it go. Aradel oozed over the top of the dome and enveloped Thane in a layer of jelly. Thane collapsed in a writhing heap struggling to free himself from the mano. Aradel quickly changed to his near-solid form, binding Thane.

David stepped forward. Aradel had captured Thane. His heart, which had been thumping in his ears, subsided to a low rumble. The hand holding the wand dropped to his side. Houdin was almost beside himself with happiness, "He's been stopped. Aradel was fantastic. The element of surprise beats careful planning every time. Find something to bind him so that Aradel can release him."

David moved toward the tattered curtains, intending to use them as ropes when suddenly Aradel cried out. David spun around to find all of Aradel's eyes were wide with pain. Thane was struggling to stand up. Through the near-solid jelly-like covering of Aradel's body David could see that Thane was slashing away at Aradel from inside, using Kira's knife.

Kira, who was just getting to her feet, reacted instantly and ran forward to tackle Thane. Pieces of Aradel began to fall to the ground as Thane hacked away. Aradel was forced to release the enraged weaver and collapsed in a heap next to the glowing dome.

Kira jumped on Thane and together the two of them rolled on the ground, Kira struggling for the wand while trying to avoid the slashing knife. David watched as the knife rose and fell. Kira cried out and rolled away from Thane, clutching her side. Blood oozed between her fingers. She struggled to stand against Thane again but collapsed as Thane regained his feet and turned to stare at David.

Houdin suddenly fluttered in front of him. With despair in his voice he flatly told David, "Run. We cannot win today. The element of surprise is lost and he is too powerful to face alone."

"No," David said. "This is our best chance. After this it just gets harder. Thane will grow more powerful. Remin will suffer more hardships. My world will be plagued by nightmares, you will die and the curse will continue. This may be our only chance."

Houdin fluttered upward and surveyed the scene. Sir Heads-a-lot lay against a column with his heads scattered all around him; Kira was passed out and bleeding at Thane's feet; Aradel was in several large pieces scattered near the dome behind Thane; and David stood alone, flanked by his two cats and facing the enraged Thane, who was grasping his injured arm and growling.

"We cannot win this day," Houdin pleaded. "I will not have you risk your life in this cause. What we have tried to do is noble and right but the odds are against us. There is no dishonor in retreat."

David swallowed his fear and tried to calm himself. "I can't leave my friends with him. Kira is hurt and needs help and Aradel and Sir Heads-a-lot deserve better than to be left in pieces. He was not expecting us thanks to Spud and Cutie. That's an advantage for us. I need to try. My parents would understand."

The time for discussion ended abruptly as Thane hissed at the two cats. Both of them bolted from David's side and disappeared into the shadows. Before David could react, Thane muttered a spell, and a ball of spectrum erupted from the end of his wand and sped toward David like a bullet. The ball hit David in the stomach and he felt intense pain as the ball drilled into him.

He doubled over, but as he did he saw the healing amulet beginning to glow. The sunstone and the moonstone began spinning and David felt warmth spreading downward from the amulet toward the cut in his stomach. He immediately felt better and watched the spectrum ball collapse and flutter to the ground. The amulet saved my life, he thought in amazement. If I weren't wearing it, Thane would have won. Instead we still have a chance.

Thane glared angrily at the amulet. David straightened up and then began to move toward the center of the room as Thane watched silently with narrowed eyes.

Thane readied his next attack and aimed his wand at David. But just as he began his spell, Cutie and Spud appeared at his feet and leaping up, began climbing him as if he were a tree. Their claws scratched deeply into the weaver and caused his arm to jerk downward in agony. The floor between them heaved as the misdirected spell blew a hole in the stone and showered David with dust and pebbles. Thane cursed and whirled around. The two cats leaped away from the enraged man and vanished again into the shadows of a broken column. "You have lasted longer than Houdin," Thane growled, "but that's not saying much. He was no match for me and neither are you or your meddling cats."

David looked at a large piece of rock on the floor in front of Thane. He hoped that his wand had enough earth spectrum to accomplish the spell he was thinking of. He aimed his wand at the rock and said, "Terra nullgravium." His wand grew warm in his hands as green and silver spectrum shot out of the end and enveloped the rock. The rock rose off of the floor and headed straight for Thane but Thane was quick. With his own wand he performed the same spell and his rock leaped up to intercept David's.

The stream of spectrum from David's wand stopped just as the two rocks met in the middle of the floor and slammed together, pulverizing both boulders and showering David, Thane and Kira with the shattered pieces. Thane and David both ducked down to avoid the shower of stone while Kira moaned and covered her head with her hands.

David moved quickly as the dust cleared from the last

attack. As he moved, he readied his mind to use the Dragonium spell. He concentrated on imagining that his wand was a dragon breathing fire. He raised his wand and said, "Dragonium," as he pointed his wand at Thane. A jet of fiery red spectrum shot from the end of his wand, ignited into a burst of flame and sped with unerring accuracy toward Thane.

But Thane was more than ready for this spell. As the spectrum became flame, he raised his own wand and spoke fiercely, "Aqueous." A swirl of shimmering blue spectrum poured from his wand and transformed into water droplets, which rushed together to quench the flames reaching for him.

Just then, a blur of movement caught the corner of David's eye. He watched in amazement as one of the basins on the wall erupted, spraying water into the air. Fred came barreling out of the fountain of water and raced to intercept the water pouring from Thane's wand. A second eruption from the opposite basin revealed Michelle as she soared through the air. Fred and Michelle intercepted the stream of water. They opened their mouths as wide as they could and caught the stream. The water hit them both with the force of a fire hose bowling them over and knocking them gasping to the floor. But they had accomplished their goal and interrupted Thane's stream. The spray of water abruptly stopped and fell as harmless drops to splatter on the dusty floor.

David's fire spout, with nothing to stop it, hit the hem of Thane's robes, setting them on fire. He stamped at the fire, cursing and fuming. "How many friends do you have?"

While Thane attempted to extinguish his burning robes, David raced forward, scooped up the two serpents and tossed them into the nearest basin with a splash. "Thanks," he called out as two tails jutted out of the basin and then vanished with a practiced flip.

Thane extinguished the fire and then moved toward the dome. David ran toward the mirror on the wall. Houdin was undone by a mirror like this, he thought. If I am in front of it, Thane can't use it against me.

"Good idea! Don't give him any advantage," counseled

Houdin, who was flying behind David to avoid the flames.

David found himself looking into the dome where a miniature version of the Imaginator was assembled. A rusty pile of pipes served as a stand for the four power crystals and the rainbow prism. On the floor under the stand was the spectrum stone, glowing with immense power. Smoky white air filled the dome. A stream of spectrum sputtered out of the hole in the top.

Houdin flew over to the dome and his voice came through loud and clear in David's mind. "Well, it's not perfect. The alignment between the crystals and the prism is inaccurate so the spectrum output is poor, but he's got it working."

Thane aimed his wand at David, but at that moment Queenie attacked with a ferocious growl. Thane shifted and aimed a stream of spectrum toward the leaping animal. The spectrum struck Queenie in midair. Her growl ceased; she was frozen. She dropped like a stone to the floor and landed with a crash, falling amid the rubble. David could hear Kira moaning in pain and grief.

Thane then turned toward the dome. "Fear will be your undoing," he crowed and held up his wand, pointing the weaving spool toward the top of the dome. He began chanting. The spool glowed and spun. The spectrum streaming out of the dome steadied, flowed toward the spool and swirled around it in a miniature tornado of power. David was puzzled. He wasn't asleep. Thane couldn't terrorize his dreams. But in that instant, the evil weaver's intent became clear. The meld with Houdin broke as David's mind filled with images that terrified him. He saw his parents in pain and screaming and he couldn't help them. His leg tingled and he saw blood begin to pour out of a large gash. He blinked. His heart pounded and sweat dripped down his face.

He's found a way to affect people's minds while they are awake, David realized with horror. He's more dangerous than ever. My world will be destroyed.

The images kept coming—monsters grabbing him while he slept; being held underwater and not being able to breathe. He felt himself panicking. The hand holding the wand was shaking. He put his hand behind his back and grasped it with the other hand to steady it. He didn't want Thane to see that his attack was having the desired effect.

Thane could feel the fear pouring out of David. The air around the boy grew hazy and Thane inhaled the scent of fear. This was so much better than using the fear he caused in the dream streams. He grew stronger as he poured every hurtful thing he could imagine into David. The spectrum stream pouring from the dome grew stronger and brighter as David's emotions went out of control.

David was unprepared for this much horror. He sagged in despair as Thane crushed his spirit without even touching him. His own mind was being used against him; and in that moment he found the key that he needed to fight back. It was his mind, not Thane's. He controlled his own perceptions.

Slowly, so that Thane would not be alerted, he began to take control of the images flooding into his brain. He took the image of himself drowning and inhaled deeply. As the air filled his lungs, the image shattered and vanished. He kept his eyes down, not looking at Thane, and concentrated on the gash in his leg. It's not there he thought. He looked at his bleeding leg and noticed that the healing amulet was not activated. I can't be hurt or the amulet would be working. What I think is blood pouring down my leg is just sweat. The gash in his leg closed and the blood became clear. David blinked and saw beads of sweat dripping down his leg. He replaced the picture of his screaming parents with an image of the three of them snuggled in a big bed reading bedtime stories. The panic he was feeling began to lift. If Thane could have seen his face, he would have seen David concentrating as hard as he could, with a slight smile beginning to appear on his face.

Thane was blinded by ecstasy. He didn't see the stream of spectrum begin to falter on its path to his wand. He didn't see the light within the Imaginator as it fluctuated and dimmed. His eyes were closed as he inhaled the scent of fear filling the room.

David could feel the panic inside him beginning to ease.

Thane kept sending more images to his brain but he pushed them aside and regained control. He couldn't keep this up forever. Thane would figure it out soon enough and then things would be even worse than they already were. He began to think about all that Houdin had taught him. The only fire spell he had ever used was the Dragonium spell and that one obviously wouldn't help him now. His mind wandered through the spell books that he had been looking at. He could see each page in his mind and he dismissed most of the spells because they weren't appropriate or they were too complex.

The only spell that seemed even remotely helpful was the Solarius spell. If he remembered it correctly, the spell produced a beam of heat similar to the sun shining through a magnifying glass. He wracked his brain, trying to figure out a way to use this spell against Thane, even as he continued to block the nightmarish images that kept coming. Just when he began to despair it came to him. He almost laughed out loud. I hope this works, he thought.

Thane began to sense the failure of power over David's mind. He opened his eyes to glare at the boy, who was standing with his head bowed in apparent defeat, his hands behind his back.

David was murmuring to himself, trying to maintain some kind of self-control.

Thane's face contorted with hate as he sent more images toward David. The spectrum flow steadied as he focused his power again.

David looked sideways at the dome as he began the Solarius spell. His wand was behind his back pointing at the mirror. He could feel the wand begin to get warmer in his hands. He pushed Thane's images away and replaced them with the image of the beam of heat bouncing off the mirror, going through the glass dome and hitting the stand holding the crystals. As he gazed through half-closed eyes at the stand, he saw a spot on it begin to glow and turn red. He shifted the spot to the metal near the fire crystal and poured all his concentration into the spell. In seconds, the metal was red-hot and the post holding the crystal began to sag as it melted. As soon as David saw the crystal sag downward he shifted the beam to the next crystal.

Thane's concentration broke as the stream of power from the dome shifted. The stream of spectrum surged outward and began to spiral around him. In an instant Thane found himself inside a tornado of spectrum. He screamed. He didn't understand what was happening. The tornado tightened around him. The power of the spectrum began to spiral upward.

Thane was furious. He struggled to regain control of the spectrum but it was as if someone else was controlling it. He looked at David and saw that something had changed. The eyes that had earlier registered defeat now were blue and sparkling and there was a slight smile on his face.

David looked up and watched the tornado of spectrum continue to climb upward around Thane. As it rose to his waist, Thane raised his wand over his head struggling to keep his power. The spectrum swirled around his face. Thane screamed. The spectrum tornado began to glow, and in an instant it exploded. David was thrown against a broken column, striking the back of his head with a loud "thunk." His thoughts were on Thane. I've killed him. I've never killed anyone before but there was no other way. He heard the clatter of Thane's wand as it fell to the floor and felt immense sadness as everything faded to black.

14 ∗ HOMEWARD BOUND

"David, can you hear me?" David drifted back into consciousness. He could hear an insistent purring in his ears. He slowly opened his eyes. Kira lay next to him, gently slapping his face. Cutie and Spud sat purring on either side of him. Houdin hovered above him, making frantic circles. I must not have been out for very long, he thought. Small stones were still clattering to the floor from the explosion-damaged ceiling, and dust mixed with spectrum hung heavy in the air. David sat up, rubbing the back of his head with one hand and holding his wand with the other.

Everything that had just happened came flooding back as David shook his head, trying to clear the effects of the explosion. Grief filled him as images of Aradel, Sir Heads-a-lot, and even Thane flashed through his mind. He had lost two good friends and he had been responsible for Thane's death. Kira's face blurred in front of him as his eyes welled up with tears.

"Thank goodness, you're all right," moaned Kira. She was still doubled up and holding her side.

Just then, the fluttering butterfly tumbled to the ground. "Houdin!" David cried. He scrambled over to the cursed wizard but stopped when he saw the wings of the butterfly fall off. "What's happening? Is he dying?" First Sir Heads-a-lot, then Aradel, and now Houdin, thought David.

But to his amazement, the wingless butterfly began growing and transforming in a blaze of light. David shielded his eyes. The light dimmed and he saw a man in a white robe, hunched over on all fours, with his long hair hiding his face. For one awful moment, David thought that Thane had returned but then the head lifted and David saw Houdin for the first time. The wizard's face was beaming with a smile that seemed to fill the whole room.

Houdin got unsteadily to his feet. "You did it, David. You defeated Thane and," he patted at his robes, "you have restored me to my old and magical self."

"Yes, but I had to kill Thane to do it," agonized David. "I didn't want to kill him. I couldn't think of any other way." Tears flowed down David's cheeks.

Houdin chuckled. "David, he's not dead. Although he might soon wish that he was." He came over and knelt down so that his face was even with David's. "When Thane realized that an explosion was imminent he tried to think of a way to save himself. There were many good ways but he was so confused by the turn of events that he could only think of one. He cursed himself with the reincarnation spell. Now he's in your world as a caterpillar egg." Houdin's voice was full of mirth. He stood up. "Of course we will have to be on our guard in case he finds a way to return to Remin, but we are forewarned. When and if he returns, things will be different here."

"Different?" asked David.

Houdin moved over to Kira and began examining her wound. "Yes. Thane may not have done it the right way, but it is now obvious that Remin needs to find other ways to do things without a total reliance on spectrum." Sighing, he turned and walked across the floor to pick up Thane's wand. He removed the spool and slipped it into his robes. He examined the wand and then approached Kira. He touched her wound with Thane's wand and said, "Coagulatius." The wand glowed and David watched in amazement as the edges of the knife wound began to close like a zipper. In an instant the skin was whole again. The only sign of the injury that was left was the rip in her shirt and the blood that had soaked her clothing.

David exclaimed, "If you can do that, then you can heal Sir Heads-a-lot!"

Houdin shook his head, "No, there are limitations to all magic and especially when it comes to healing magic. I can help Kira because I understand her body structure. I can imagine the steps to take to stop bleeding and repair organs." He moved across the room to examine Sir Heads-a-lot. "Sir Heads-a-lot is a mystery to me. I can't heal something that I don't understand." He shook his head ruefully as he looked at the scattered heads near the body.

David's heart sank. So much was going right that his hopes had soared, thinking that all of Thane's damage could be reversed. He walked over to join Houdin. He gazed at his headless friend and tears streamed down his face. He sank down on the floor and hugged the headless body, silently for his lost friend. As he stared at Sir Heads-a-lot, a tiny button-sized head fell out of one of the pockets. He reached out to catch it and found himself holding head number one, Sir Heads-a-lot's own face. He placed the head back on Sir Heads-a-lot's shoulders and gently lowered the body back to the floor. He turned and began slowly gathering up the remaining heads that had spilled onto the floor.

Houdin stared at Thane's wand. "I wish I had my own wand. It's a little creepy to use Thane's." He grimaced.

Kira sat up and began rummaging through a pack, muttering to herself. "All you had to do was ask," she said, and with a flourish she pulled a glass wand from the pack and handed it to the astonished wizard. "Ta-da!" She laughed. "I brought it along on the slim hope that I would get the chance to give it back to you. I picked it up after Thane cursed you."

Houdin took the wand and looked at it lovingly. David saw that Houdin's wand had more curves in it but it still had the same beautiful smoky look that his own wand had. Houdin's face wore a huge grin as he twirled his own wand with authority and pocketed Thane's wand. He smiled and winked at David.

"I can use any wand, but with my own wand I have much better control and therefore greater power." David watched the newly restored wizard walk across the room and bend over Aradel. After examining the motionless form for a moment, Houdin shook his head sadly. He turned to look at David but his eyes widened and shifted as he yelled out, "David, look behind you."

David turned around. The head he had placed on Sir Heads-a-lot had grown to its normal size. The eyes opened and both hands came rose up to adjust the head. Sir Heads-a-lot sat up and looked around. His hands began searching the floor for lost heads. David rushed over and poured the heads into his friend's outstretched hands.

"You're alive. I can't believe it!" exclaimed David.

"Well, apparently it's no easier to kill me here than it is in Inspire. In Inspire I could grow a new head but here it looks like I just need my original head to get me going again," said Sir Heads-a-lot. "I didn't know that but now that I've found out, I'll have to be more careful." His hands moved rapidly, sorting and replacing all his many heads into their appropriate pockets. As he worked, he asked, "What happened?"

David, Houdin and Kira gathered around him and in a clatter of conflicting stories, brought Sir Heads-a-lot up to date. When David talked about Queenie's attack, Houdin got up and walked over to the frozen statue. After a quick examination, he waved his wand. Blue, green and silver spectrum rose off the statue and returned to the wand, lifting the ice particles from Queenie's fur. Her pelt returned to its natural blue-gray color and moments later she shook violently, ran exuberantly over to Kira, and began slobbering all over her face. Kira laughed and petted her enthusiastic friend.

David continued telling Sir Heads-a-lot his story. He concluded with his blackout, and then Houdin picked up the rest of the story of Thane's defeat. Just as they finished their summary, Queenie bolted from Kira's side and headed for the doorway where she began howling frantically. They all turned to the doorway and watched the stone portal slide silently aside. A group of mano glided into the room, but halted when confronted by Queenie, who was growling deep in her throat. Every one of the mano held some kind of weapon. David saw spears, swords, a mace, and a length of chain. Two of the mano held blazing torches. Houdin, Kira, and Sir Heads-a-lot gathered around David. Houdin, now clearly in command of the little group, pushed David behind him and with a swirl of his cloak and confronted the approaching mob with upraised wand. Kira scooped up her sword and joined him. Sir Heads-a-lot exchanged his head for a lion head and with a roar joined the group to confront the mano.

The two groups advanced towards each other and met in the middle of the room. The leader of the mano stepped forward and gestured for everyone to stop. He broke into a large smile, "Thane's hold on us has been broken. We are now free and we desire to help."

The mano moved forward and gathered around Aradel. The leader of the mano separated himself from the group and moved back to converse in low tones with Houdin. After a few moments, he rejoined the group surrounding the pieces of Aradel. They conversed quietly, and then as David watched all of the mano melted into a puddle on the floor. Aradel's body was engulfed by the wave of jelly. David could see eyes, lungs and other assorted organs all mixed together in the pool of jelly. Aradel's body was no longer visible. It was mixed with all the other mano. And then, just as quickly as they had melted, the mano reformed but now Aradel stood among them.

"Aradel!" David rushed forward.

Aradel smiled and waved. He thanked his fellow mano and then came over to rejoin Kira, David, Sir Heads-a-lot and Houdin. "It's good to see you again, Houdin. You have obviously been successful. I am eager to hear your story."

Houdin grinned. "And we are eager to hear your story as well."

Before they could continue, Kira sat down and began shivering. Houdin looked alarmed. "She's in shock from loss of blood. We need to keep her warm." Queenie rushed over and began licking her face. The lion fiddled with his head and Sir Heads-a-lot reappeared. He helped Kira lay down and elevated her feet on some of the rubble in the room.

David rushed over and pulled the tattered curtains down. He wrapped the curtains around Kira's shoulders. He then hurried to Thane's table (or what was left of it after the explosion). He piled the broken boards together and pulled out his wand. A quick Dragonium spell and the wood was soon blazing and spreading warmth over the entire room. He removed the healing amulet from around his neck and placed it over Kira's head. The moon stone and sun stone began spinning and the central stone began to glow with a soft humming sound. Kira soon stopped shivering and Queenie settled down. Kira began stroking Queenie's head, which rested in her lap.

Aradel stayed as far away from the fire as possible. Kira took some food from their supplies and everyone settled down to eat and catch up with what had happened.

Aradel began his story. "There's not a whole lot to tell. When the cobralan attacked, I made myself as small as possible to try to avoid injury, but that was a mistake because it made it easy for the beast to swallow me."

"How were you able to escape that?" David asked in amazement. The two cats were seated on their haunches on either side of him like silent sentinels.

"Yes, how did you do it?" came a pair of voices in unison. The whole group turned to find Fred and Michelle leaning forward in one of the basins so they could listen to the tales. They were both smiling and looked none the worse for wear after their little foray out of the water during the battle with Thane.

The whole group burst out laughing as Aradel, looking a little annoyed at the interruptions, continued, "I inhaled as much water as I could which caused me to swell up and choke the infernal beast." He laughed and David was amazed at the difference in his personality. All through the journey, Aradel had been sullen and bitter, not at all good company. Now with Thane defeated, the change was remarkable. David couldn't help but marvel at the change. "The cobralan coughed me up and I rushed to catch up with you in the ruins. I got lost for a while but eventually found Thane's room. The battle was already underway so I snuck into the room through one of the larger drain pipes."

"Oh, bravo. Now it's going to get crowded in the pipes if everybody uses them to get around," grumped Fred. "It's crowded enough with Michelle in there."

"Hey, are you calling me fat?" joshed Michelle. She turned away from Fred in a pretend snit but as Fred circled around to look in her face, she laughed and playfully pushed him.

"The rest of it, you already know," Aradel concluded.

The meal was soon finished and Kira packed up the remaining food. She was almost back to her old self. The healing amulet stopped spinning and glowing, indicating that it couldn't help anymore, so she removed the amulet and gave it back to David. "Thanks, you probably saved my life. You are one special young man." She tousled his hair and David looked away, embarrassed at the attention. Houdin and David found Thane's supply of spectrum and used it to reload their wands and refill their sacks.

They now turned their attention to the Imaginator. The explosion had destroyed the glass dome that had protected Thane from the power within. Now, with the quinquetal melted by David's spell, and the crystals and prism scattered by the explosion, the Imaginator was cold and lifeless. Houdin took the torn curtains and used them to carefully wrap each piece. The spectrum stone still retained a dim glow. Houdin used Kira's walking stick to roll it onto a piece of curtain. He then carefully wrapped it in several layers of curtain material. He asked the mano guards to find a container and they returned with several wooden boxes and a large wooden chest. Houdin put the spectrum stone in a wooden box and placed the box in the chest. David had gathered up the four crystals. "Keep the prism away from the crystals," warned Houdin, "It's going to be safest if we keep the pieces out of the light and separated."

David brought the crystals to Houdin who wrapped each one in its own piece of curtain and placed it in a box, which he then added to the chest. The rainbow prism came last. With all the pieces of the Imaginator packed in the chest and all their supplies packed up again, the group was finally ready to leave. Sir Heads-a-lot offered to carry the chest, but Houdin's eyes twinkled as he casually waved his wand, releasing a spurt of spectrum. David watched in amazement, for under Houdin's control, the spectrum seemed almost alive. The swirling glitter reached out and enveloped the chest, which floated off the floor as if cradled in a pair of gentle hands. Kira smiled at David's open-mouthed awe and gave him a glance that seemed to say, "I told you so." Houdin headed for the doorway and the chest followed behind like an eager puppy.

Fred and Michelle put on their widest grins as they watched the chest bobbing across the room. They waved to everyone, said good-bye, and vanished down the basin.

With one last look at the ruined room of the vanquished weaver, the group all moved through the ruins retracing their course. The mano guards split up, with half taking the lead and the rest watching the rear. Kira followed with Houdin and David and the two cats walking in the middle. Aradel was in the back with the mano.

David was exhausted. I'm not looking forward to the journey back to Remin, he thought. It's too bad we can't use magic to get back. He had asked Houdin about it but Houdin explained that while he might have been able to get himself back to Remin, transporting a group of mano, plus Kira, Sir Heads-a-lot, David, Aradel, and two cats was too difficult to accomplish. Hopefully, Houdin would be able to help them traverse Lake Istep and avoid the cobralan. The only bright side to the whole trip was that they didn't have to sneak around to avoid Thane's spies, so they should be able to travel much faster.

They made their way through the hallways and corridors of Salvar, which was now eerily silent, and soon were standing outside staring at the lake. The floating chest began to slowly sink to the ground as the spell weakened, but Houdin barely glanced at it as he flicked his wand while muttering under his breath, and the chest bobbed into the air again. David was beginning to understand why Houdin was the master wizard in Remin.

Houdin had only taken one step when Kira stopped him, pointed at the ground, and said one word, "Quicksand."

Houdin examined the ground, gauged the distance to the beach and rolled up his sleeves. He made a sweeping gesture with his wand and David distinctly heard him say, "Desicatium." The stream of spectrum that shot from his wand spread out and outlined a path that went all the way across the quicksand to the beach. David actually had to shield his eyes from the flare of power that erupted over the ground. When he opened his eyes he saw steam rising up in front of him, and his mouth fell open again as he watched the ground harden and begin to crack until it resembled a sun baked desert. Houdin smiled and gestured with his hand for everyone to cross. The little group walked single file across the now harmless quicksand, and soon arrived at the beach. The floating chest bobbed up and down next to Houdin until the spell ran out and it settled onto the sand.

They all relaxed at the edge of the lake while Houdin surveyed their position and plotted their next move. Houdin conferred with Sir Heads-a-lot who waded into the lake and switched heads, transforming himself in a large flat-headed fish with two long tentacles. The fish was the size of a large whale. David wondered why they hadn't thought of this on the way in. Sir Heads-a-lot was too big to be eaten by the cobralan so they could get all the way across the lake in one swift trip, avoiding the sink stones.

They loaded all their supplies and clambered onto the back of Sir Heads-a-lot, who rapidly moved out onto the lake. The water made both cats very nervous so David sat down and held Cutie and Spud in his lap. He relaxed, watched the blue sky and reveled in the warmth of the sun beating down on the group as they cruised across the lake toward the distant shores of Doorcliff. Now this is the way to travel, thought David.

Suddenly, Kira pointed into the water and David was startled to see the cobralan gliding underneath of them and watching them. Under the water it looked bigger than Sir Heads-a-lot and the whole group readied themselves for an attack. But it didn't attack. They were all puzzled. Was the cobralan waiting until they were close to shore before going after them, or was it somehow scared of the big fish they were traveling on? They couldn't answer the question so they settled into an uneasy silence and watched the cobralan zigzag back and forth across their path.

David was found himself worrying about Fred and Michelle. How had they avoided the cobralan earlier, and how were they going to avoid it now? He scanned the water looking for the little serpents and was disappointed that he couldn't find them. Just when he was ready to give up, he glanced behind them and saw both serpents sitting on the back of the fish and rolling with the gentle up and down motion of the tail. They turned, smiled and laughed and dipped their tails into the wake being left by their travels through the lake.

"This is the life," enthused Michelle.

"Yes, I'm so glad I thought of it," winked Fred. Michelle leaned over and gave him a little kiss. David turned back with a big grin on his face to watch the cliffs approaching and the sink stones disappearing behind them.

They landed at the base of the cliffs and unloaded their supplies. Sir Heads-a-lot used the tentacles to switch heads and reappeared as himself, wading out of the lake and shaking the water off of him like a large dog. Houdin seemed to be everywhere, making things easy for them with spectrum power. He sent a wave of warm air to wash over Sir Heads a Lot, drying him instantly. He lit a large fire to keep them all warm, and then went off to talk with Kira about the next phase of their journey.

While they were waiting to continue, David stared across the lake at Salvar. It didn't look nearly as dark and foreboding as it had when he had first seen it. The water in the lake suddenly began to bubble and froth and David rapidly stepped back in alarm. The whole party scuttled back from the waters' edge and watched as the cobralan's head and eyes emerged. Houdin stepped forward with his wand raised to defend against the inevitable attack. They were all surprised when the cobralan rolled onto its side so that its mouth was out of the water.

"Are you the ones responsible for my release from Thane's control?"

Houdin beckoned for David to step forward. David moved over next to Houdin, who placed his arm around his shoulder and said to the cobralan, "Yes, we all participated but David was the one who was finally able to break Thane's hold on other creatures, including you."

"Then I am immensely grateful to you and would like to find some way to repay you," said the cobralan. "Thane has forced me to guard the lake against my own nature. I fought him for as long as I could, but he just grew stronger and stronger and I despaired of ever finding a way to break his control. I am in your debt." The cobralan inclined its head while looking right at David.

Houdin's hand tightened on David's shoulder. "We are returning to Remin City, which lies to the northwest. If you know of any way to ease our trip over these cliffs…" He turned and made a sweeping motion with his arm to encompass the towering stone above them.

The cobralan's head swung upward to survey the cliffs. "I believe I can help you, not only to traverse the cliffs, but to get to Remin City."

The cobralan rolled back over and began moving forward toward the shore where they waited. More and more of its body emerged from the lake. David noticed that it walked on six legs with large finned feet. As its fins cleared the water, the cobralan surprised them all when it snapped its back fin upright and began flapping two pairs of enormous side fins. The breeze from the fins grew stronger and stronger. Moments later the cobralan soared up into the sky all the way to the top of the cliff and then returned to hover over the astonished group, who were staring upward, open-mouthed. David had trouble staying on his feet. The wind from the flapping fins was so strong that he stumbled backward, and eventually he had to kneel down in order to avoid being knocked over. Spud and Cutie cowered next to him. He wrapped his arms around the cats in order to keep them from being blown into the lake.

The cobralan hovered for another instant and then moved off and settled on the beach nearby. Houdin, David and the rest ran up the beach. "That's a pretty neat trick," enthused Houdin. "I never heard that cobralan could fly."

"Well, we're more comfortable in the water but it certainly helps when we want to relocate. I usually only fly at night, so that I can't be seen. But this seems like a special occasion and so I have revealed my secret to you," said the cobralan. "I will be very happy to fly you all back to the place you call Remin City. It will require multiple trips but it would please me greatly if you would accept."

Houdin glanced at the group who were all nodding enthusiastically and smiled. "I think I speak for all of us. We accept your offer. It has been a long and difficult journey and we are all tired."

They split themselves into two groups. Houdin, David, Kira, Aradel, Sir Heads-a-lot, the two cats, Queenie, and one of the mano guards arranged for the first trip. The cobralan lowered its rear four feet and the group clambered onto its back with their supplies. Houdin floated up the wooden chest containing the Imaginator pieces and Sir Heads-a-lot secured it against the upright sail fin. David placed the cats inside his jacket with their heads staring out. It was a tight fit but it was the best way for them to travel. Kira ran a rope completely around the cobralan's body to use as a handhold during the flight. When everything was secured, everyone grabbed hold of the rope and Houdin said, "We are ready."

The cobralan rose and began flapping the enormous side fins. Kira wrapped one arm around Queenie as they soared up the cliff face. David closed his eyes against the wind rushing over his face. He opened them as the flight leveled off, and watched Doorcliff rush by below them. The cobralan flew faster and faster. Houdin called out instructions, and before long the cornfields of Remin appeared beside the whirlpool lake. David could see the shadow of the cobralan reflected on the lake as they soared over it, climbed the walls of Remin City and circled the town center. Below them, David could see people looking up at the cobralan and pointing.

The cobralan hovered over the empty dome for a moment and then settled down next to it. Its gill covers were heaving wildly. Obviously it was quite a lot of work to ferry them from Lake Istep to Remin. They quickly dismounted from the cobralan as a crowd began to gather on the edges of the plaza. As soon as they were all on the ground the cobralan moved over to the fountain and took a deep drink. When it was done, the fountain was empty.

David moved up close to the cobralan. "Thank you so much."

The cobralan looked at him and said, "It is a small thing. I am glad to do it. I will retrieve the rest of your party in short order." It rested for a moment and then after insuring that everyone had moved back, took off again and soared away for his second trip.

Houdin was welcomed heartily by many of the people in the crowd. He acknowledged their greetings but his concentration was on the wooden chest that Kira and Sir Heads-a-lot were carrying. He opened the wooden chest and David wandered over to watch. Aradel slid under the door of the dome and emerged moments later through the now open door. Houdin was now looking at the dome with a grim look on his face.

"What's wrong?" said David.

"Well, we can't just put the Imaginator back into the dome. When we reassemble it and it is reactivated, anyone inside the dome will be destroyed."

David removed the healing amulet. "Will this help?"

Houdin smiled sadly while shaking his head. "Yes, but

not enough. Folin wore one and was still destroyed. We will need to consider carefully how to proceed. I've thought about this a lot and I think that I have the best chance of putting things back the way they were."

Kira stared at Houdin with an alarmed expression on her face. "There has to be another way. It's too dangerous. You are not expendable. It would be better if someone else made the attempt." She stomped her foot for emphasis, clearly believing that she should be that someone, and stood in the doorway as if she intended to block anyone from entering. Houdin sighed, gently took her arm and walked out of earshot. David watched them talking animatedly, with Kira gesturing wildly and Houdin trying to sway her to his side. Aradel glided over after a moment and joined in the conversation as well.

David watched them talking, and idly put the healing amulet back on as he thought about the dilemma that they now faced. The crowd of people were pressing in on Houdin, Kira and Aradel and staring at the six wrapped objects while murmuring to themselves. David could see in many of their faces that the lack of spectrum had been very hard on them. Some people looked gaunt and underfed. Others had dark sunken eyes as if they were not getting enough sleep. But as David looked from face to face, he could see that there was a hint of hope on each face. They were placing all their trust in Houdin.

And Houdin was not going to disappoint them. The discussion with Kira and Aradel came to an end, and Houdin and Aradel walked back over to the doorway of the Imaginator. Kira moved off into the crowd. Houdin had a satisfied look on his face but Aradel was totally unreadable. Houdin smiled at David, "We have a plan."

The crowd moved back away from the dome at Houdin's insistence. Kira reappeared carrying a small journal, which she opened and consulted as she talked about what they had decided. She discussed the alignment of the crystals with Houdin and the placement of the rainbow prism. "Now, because we have never been able to examine the Imaginator while it is active, we have made several guesses about the alignment."

Kira knelt down and began unwrapping the Imaginator stones. "We'll save the spectrum stone for last and place all the other stones as best we can. Hopefully we can align them correctly without activating the Imaginator. Aligning the spectrum stone will be the hardest because the stone has an irregular shape. Houdin thinks all the alignment problems are solved by the crystals and the rainbow prism. We can only hope that he's right." It still seemed dangerous to David, but he stood back to watch his friends work.

Aradel took two crystals and Kira took the other two as they approached the doorway. David started to follow but Houdin reached out and stopped him.

"You've done enough already. While this part should not be dangerous, I couldn't live with myself if something happened to you. You'll have to wait here." He looked into David's eyes and waited until David nodded slowly. Then he reached down, picked up the rainbow prism and followed Kira and Aradel into the Imaginator.

David watched from the doorway as Kira and Aradel placed the crystals on the quinquetal. Sir Heads-a-lot had stayed back from the discussion but now he leaned over David's head and watched the activity inside the dome. Houdin watched carefully and made several suggestions, then he helped them align the crystals in their holders. When Houdin was finally satisfied, he placed the rainbow prism carefully at the top. They returned and began unwrapping the glowing spectrum stone. The murmuring of the crowd died away as Houdin took out his wand, approached the stone and began murmuring quietly to himself.

"What now?" David asked Houdin, but Kira hurriedly pulled him aside. "Don't disturb him. He's going to try and float the spectrum stone into place from the doorway. If he's successful we can seal the door as the Imaginator is activated and no one will be hurt."

"That's a great plan!" David said enthusiastically and stepped back to watch Houdin's attempt. Aradel stood by, ready to seal the door, while Kira began pacing nervously. Houdin looked from the stone to the area under the quinquetal several times and then he began his spell, murmuring softly and waving the wand in slow circles over the glowing stone. David was staring at the stone so hard he almost missed it. Houdin flicked his wand toward the stone and a stream of silver spectrum shot out. But the power of the spectrum never touched the stone. A bright flash and a tremendous explosion suddenly filled the plaza. Houdin was blasted backward through the air, landing limply on the cobblestones surrounding the dome.

15 * THE REMIN PLAZA

The blast knocked David and Sir Heads-a-lot down and slammed Kira against the dome wall. Aradel was thrown into the open doorway and soon emerged, brushing himself off. He hurried over to Houdin as Kira groaned and struggled to her feet. She gasped as she took in the scene and ran to join Aradel, who was bending over the wizard. David and Sir Heads-a-lot joined them moments later.

Aradel stood up. "He's unconscious and it looks like his arm is broken."

Kira's hair obscured the wizard's face as she bent over him. David turned to Aradel. "What happened?"

Aradel shook his head. "I'm not sure but it would appear that you can't use spectrum power on the spectrum stone. We're going to have to find another way."

Sir Heads-a-lot was rubbing his neck and staring at the fallen wizard. "Is there anything I can do to help?" He took a hasty step backward as Kira suddenly jerked upright.

Kira stood up quickly and David could see her eyes blazing with a new energy. "I will make the attempt. Houdin should never have risked himself." She turned to David and held out her hand. "Give me the healing amulet and I will place the stone."

David stepped back in shock. Aradel glided over. "She's right. Houdin tried and it is not his power that can fix this. She will make the attempt, and if she fails, I will try to complete what she starts."

With trembling fingers, David removed the amulet and handed it to Kira. He was trying to think of another way, but everything was moving so fast. It still didn't seem right to him but he didn't have any better ideas.

Kira put on the amulet, and with some difficulty she hefted the spectrum stone. The healing amulet flickered in the proximity of the stone. Already Kira was being affected. Aradel went to the doorway and waited as Kira moved past him and entered the dome. Aradel closed the door behind her. David nervously took up his position beside Aradel to watch through the window in the door.

Kira placed the stone right at the edge of the depression, adjusted it, and then as David watched intently, she took a deep breath, pushed the spectrum stone into position and hurriedly stepped back. As soon as the stone settled into its place, it brightened, and shafts of power shot upward toward the crystals as a faltering hum filled the dome.

David saw that the Imaginator was not properly aligned. The power emanating from the stone was not properly focused and waves of color were splashing all over the dome instead of being directed into the rainbow prism. Kira shielded her eyes from the intense glow but the faltering hum that filled the room told her what she needed to know and she stepped forward to move one of the crystals. The hum grew stronger as the crystal fell into position and a solid line of color extended from the crystal to the prism. The glow grew stronger and Kira stumbled to her knees. David gasped. The healing stone couldn't overcome the immense power of the Imaginator, even when it was only partially working. Without even thinking, he started forward but Aradel blocked his path.

"My duty here is clear. You are not to be risked and she must be allowed to try and finish. If she falters, I will make the attempt. My brother brought us to this place. It is my place to restore the Imaginator and redeem my family's honor." David glanced over at Sir Heads-a-lot hoping for some support but the tall man just let his eyes drop. David would get no help there.

David sagged and watched as Aradel stared through the window in the door. After a long moment Aradel spoke softly. "She has adjusted the second crystal but she is faltering. She may not succeed." Almost before he finished speaking he oozed under the door and plunged into the glowing interior. David could see Kira slumped in a heap next to the Imaginator. Three of the crystals were aligned and the hum of power was much stronger. Aradel grabbed Kira and began pulling her out. Halfway across the room, he sagged slightly but then straightened and continued to the doorway. Moments later he dragged Kira free and the door swung slowly closed behind him.

Aradel gasped for air and slumped over Kira. The healing amulet was completely black. David could see that Kira was still alive but her breathing was very shallow, and soon he couldn't even see her as Sir Heads-a-lot bent over and several people in the crowd pushed forward to help. David was pushed back against the wall of the Imaginator.

David stared at the knot of people surrounding his friends. There was another group gathered around Houdin, and a man that David assumed was a doctor was working on the wizard's arm. They have already endured so much, he thought. They don't deserve to suffer anymore. Maybe the Imaginator can be activated without destroying anyone. He didn't know if it could be done but after all the impossible things he had already seen, it wasn't hard to imagine. Maybe the problem is that the people here can't imagine surviving. They have spent their whole lives believing that the power in the dome will destroy them. Folin entered the dome believing that the only thing between him and destruction was the healing amulet. Once the amulet failed, he was already resigned to his fate. I don't have that kind of belief to hinder me, he thought.

He eyed the dome. The more he looked at it and the people surrounding it, the more he believed that he might be right. Imagination is so powerful in this world and I have already proved that my imagination can make me a pretty good wizard, if I do say so myself. Inwardly he grinned. But what if I'm wrong? That thought sobered him up quickly. What if I enter the dome and it does kill me?

He looked around at his friends. They had already sacrificed so much to get this far. They had protected him and risked their lives for him many times over during this adventure. Kira, Aradel and Sir Heads-a-lot would have willingly died to save him. Thane had almost killed Kira and Aradel. That's what friendship is: a willingness to sacrifice for the people you love. It was true that he also had risked much when he confronted Thane, but he wanted to take this risk for himself as well. My parents would understand. They believed in him and they taught him to value life and help your friends. Here was another chance to help even if he might be destroyed. He tried to calm himself. His heart was pounding in his ears but he was convinced that he should do this.

Kira had told him many things during their adventure and one of those utterances came back to him as he watched the frantic activity in the plaza. She had said, "…the fact is that every single person who has ever been inside the dome for even a moment while the Imaginator is active has been destroyed. I can show you examples in my studies of scientists who have looked for only seconds from the open doorway. They were immediately blinded and died within an hour of exposure. Only the mano have shown any resistance, and they still can only handle short exposures near the doorway."

David took a deep breath, and then tried the door to the Imaginator dome. As he had hoped, it opened easily. In his haste to get Kira out, Aradel hadn't made sure that it closed enough to activate the automatic lock. David pulled open the door just enough so that he could slip through. No one noticed as he pulled the door closed behind him. He was now inside the Imaginator. David could feel sweat beginning to drip down his face and he realized that with the door closed the dome quickly became an oven, capturing the heat of the sun through the hole in the roof.

David approached the platform as quickly as he could. He shielded his eyes as he stepped onto the dais where the crystals were glowing and humming. He tried to hurry but he also wanted to make sure he did it right the first time. He glanced at the door and saw Sir Heads-a-lot's face pressed against the glass. He looked frantic.

Squinting against the bright light, David could see that somehow Kira had gotten the crystals aligned but the spectrum stone itself was unfocused. Kira was wrong, he thought, the alignment of the stone is just as important as the crystals. David shielded his eyes and listened to the hum of the crystals. The hum was loud but still unsteady. Without opening his eyes he began shifting the stone by rolling it a little at a time. After each movement he had to stop and listen to the crystals. His heart was thudding in his chest. It seemed to him that the thumping was even louder than the humming that surrounded him.

He closed his eyes tightly. I don't want to die. Even as he tried to shut out the thought of dying, he continued to shift the stone, and just when he thought he would never get it the hum of the crystals suddenly shifted and the whole room began to sing.

David's whole body was jolted by the energy of the Imaginator. He tried to imagine that he had erected a shield around himself that would protect him from the dangerous power that he had just unleashed. He felt a hot stab and he began to panic that he was burning up inside. That feeling was suddenly replaced by intense shivering and he collapsed on the dais. It felt like a spike was being driven right between his eyes. It was just like the headaches he got from drinking really cold slushies. He grasped his head and rubbed his temples trying to alleviate the pain, which vanished as quickly as it had appeared and was replaced by a feeling of complete calm. The blast furnace heat of the dome receded in the distance, and as he breathed in, his lungs filled with cool crisp air. He felt as light as a feather and his body seemed to rise off the floor. The feeling lasted only an instant, for he was suddenly slammed to the floor and he tasted sand in his mouth. He tried to spit it out but there was nothing there. As quickly as all these sensations rushed over him, they disappeared and he was left gasping in the intense heat of the power coming from the Imaginator. *I wonder if Folin felt like this before he died?*

The light was so bright that even with his eyes closed he could see the shadow of the quinquetal right through his eyelids. He lowered his head and backed slowly down from the platform toward where he thought the door was. It seemed to take forever. He kept reaching behind him with his feet, and just when he thought he must be going in a circle his foot touched the wall. He stood up and faced the wall and began inching around the dome looking for the door. He knew he was getting close when he heard Sir Heads-a-lot's voice screaming outside. "David, get out. Hurry. It's working." He moved more quickly and reached the handle on the door. "Step back. I'm coming out," he shouted. He waited a minute and then pulled the handle, opened the door a crack, slipped through and closed it.

Sir Heads-a-lot hugged him as David slowly opened his eyes and blinked at the bright sunlight. As his eyes adjusted he looked to the top of the dome and grinned broadly. A steady stream of spectrum was rising straight up and out of sight and even as he watched a few spectrum fluttered down in front of him.

The crowd around him parted and a very disheveled Houdin pushed through to get to the doorway. David could tell that his arm was no longer broken because it was tightly gripping his wand. His face was grim. "You risked more than you imagined." He glanced at the new spectrum stream and then turned a worried look back on David.

"How do you feel?" asked Houdin.

"Fine."

"Are you sure?" Houdin sounded perplexed. "Can you see me?"

"Of course I can see you."

"That's a good sign." Houdin turned and examined Aradel and Kira. With a burst of healing power, his wand restored Aradel, who had not been exposed for very long but

Kira took much longer. It took a very strong healing spell to even get her to open her eyes and moan. "I'm only able to heal her because the Imaginator was not functioning at full strength yet. If she had been successful at getting the crystals aligned, then even I couldn't have done anything to save her."

David looked around at each of his friends. The crowd was closing in again. He could see a lot of happy faces gazing up at the top of the dome and pointing. No matter what happened, he had done it. He suddenly felt very weak. He slumped down and felt unfamiliar hands grasp him under his arms and carry him to the fountain.

A small group of people had formed a fire brigade from a nearby well and was busy refilling the fountain. Someone pushed a cup of water into his hands, which he drank gratefully.

"Am I dying?"

Houdin reappeared at his side and leaned over and listened to his heart. "I don't think so. I don't know. This doesn't seem right. With the amount of time you were in the dome, I'm surprised you even got out."

David described all the sensations that had come over him inside the dome. Houdin was puzzled by his descriptions. "Folin complained that it felt like his insides were dissolving, which wasn't that far from the truth." Houdin's voice suddenly trailed away.

David closed his eyes and rested for a moment, listening to the water lapping in the fountain and the sound of the bucket brigade as they continued to refill it. He was startled by a shout and sat up so quickly that he bumped into Sir Heads-a-Lot, who was sitting next to him, and knocked him off balance. He collapsed in a heap and David helped him up, apologizing all the time. He shielded his eyes and glanced up into the sky to see the cobralan's shadow silhouetted against the bright sun. The cobralan was returning with the rest of the mano guards.

The plaza was cleared to make room for the cobralan, who circled and then settled again with his head near the fountain. The mano dismounted and David could hear the happiness of families welcoming home long lost loved ones. The cobralan moved close to the fountain and rapidly drained it again, to the dismay of the bucket brigade, who moaned good-naturedly and began refilling it again.

David was just now beginning to relax from the whole adventure. It looks like it's all coming to an end, he thought sadly. As if in answer to his thought, Fred and Michelle popped up in the shallow water of the fountain. They looked a little panicked and they both appeared to be exhausted. Fred flopped over to David. "We just got back from your house."

"My house?" asked David, as Michelle flopped over next to Fred.

Fred was leaning on the side of the fountain. "Yes, Houdin asked us to use the blue spectrum he left in the tub to help us locate your house. Well, we just came from there and we think you need to know…"

"Your parents are awake!" screamed Michelle. "You don't have much time before they realize you're missing."

The end was here. He had to get back before his parents knew he was missing. He knew how frantic they would be if he wasn't in his bed when they came upstairs to check on him. He didn't want them to be hurt but he also didn't want all this to end. He would miss all the friends he had made here and he wouldn't be a wizard anymore. There was so much more to learn and now he didn't have any more time. His friends seemed to realize he was leaving and they each came up to him to say goodbye.

Aradel shuffled up. "I didn't have much faith in you when you got here. A young boy against Thane." He shook his head. "I was wrong. You saved me. Not just fighting Thane, but in allowing me to participate in his defeat and redeem my brother from his mistake. I can't thank you enough." David wrapped his arms around Aradel's jelly-like middle.

"I'm glad I got to know you. I hope to see you again."

Sir Heads-a-Lot clattered up. "You allowed me to accompany you on the greatest adventure of my life." He enthusiastically clapped David on the back. "I was alone and despaired of ever getting back home, but you made me feel like I belong and that there will always be a place for me here."

As if to prove his point, he walked rapidly over to a group of children using a stick to try and get their ball out of a tree. Sir Heads-a-lot fumbled for a moment and then put on a squirrel head. His hands became sharp claws, which he used to rapidly climb the tree and knock the ball down to the squealing children. David watched in amusement as he walked across the plaza, changing heads and transforming himself again. Behind him the children began trying to get the ball stuck in the tree again.

Kira was carried over to him on a stretcher. Her face was white but she grinned as best she could at him. She was crying as she held out her arms and David leaned over to get a hug. She pulled the healing amulet from her neck and placed it around his. "Take this, to remember us by. I'm going to miss you a lot, little one," she whispered. "Houdin sure knows how to pick 'em. You could probably have given Houdin a run for his money in the magic department," she whispered.

"I heard that," harrumphed Houdin who had come over from observing the spectrum stream issuing from the Imaginator. "I don't like it, but she may be right." And now he was smiling. "You would have made a great wizard. I hope to see you again someday."

Now David was crying. "What's going to happen?"

Houdin patted him gently on the shoulder. "Why, just what we discussed. We'll find better and more efficient ways to use spectrum and we'll start to look for ways to do things for ourselves and decrease our reliance on the Imaginator. You've given us the time to do it and all of Remin is in your debt."

"But what about our dreams?"

"No easy answers there. We'll look at the problem. Remin would never be a party to the destruction of another world so we will continue to work with the dream streams. Maybe that's all we were really meant to use the spectrum for." Houdin looked at Fred and Michelle who were slapping their fins in the water in a show of impatience. "You need to get back. I'm fairly certain I could return you to your world, but I have no way of knowing where in your world you would end up. On the other hand, Fred and Michelle can get you right back to your house."

"What?"

"It's really fairly simple. I will transform you into a small water serpent and Fred and Michelle will guide you to your house. When you get back to your world the spell (unlike a curse) will be cancelled and you will return to your normal self." He rolled up his sleeves and took out his wand.

David said a final goodbye to his friends and then climbed into the fountain as Houdin took aim with his wand. "Goodbye, and thank you."

David had a sudden thought. "Tell the face on your door goodbye for me."

Houdin nodded, and the wizard's eyes filled with tears as he murmured, "Puffnstuff." A swirl of blue and green spectrum soon obscured David's view of his friends. The spectrum glowed brightly and fluttered to the surface of the water. David found himself staring up at his friends through the water. He could see the sadness on their faces. He looked at himself. He was a green serpent wearing a tiny jacket. Sadly he saw the healing amulet floating lazily on the bottom of the pool. It must have fallen off when he transformed. He tapped his jacket with his fin and felt his wand, still in the pocket.

Fred and Michelle swam up in front of him. "Come on, we don't have much time. We might be too late even now." They reached out with their tiny arms and grabbed David's fins. They began dragging him through the water. They reached a drainpipe and they squeezed into it single file.

David started to get scared. The pipe was dark but as they started to go down the pipe he saw that the pipe had a slight glow. As his eyes adjusted, he could clearly see where he was going. Fred's tail was waving in front of him and Michelle was pushing at him from behind. David concentrated on Fred's shape in front of him and swam as fast as he could to keep up.

He couldn't figure out how they found their way. They never hesitated even though they passed many other pipes during the trip. Right, left, right, right, up, up again, down, through a spiral of pipes that made David dizzy. He started to see objects in the pipes. Coins, rings, watches, keys. David wanted to stop and look but Michelle's insistent pushing made it impossible.

Just when he thought they must be lost, Fred began climbing up and up and up. David saw that his own fins were turning back into hands. He was back in his world but he'd better hurry or he'd transform in this pipe and he was pretty sure that wouldn't work very well.

All three of them popped out of the drain of the tub in David's bathroom. In an instant David found himself sitting in the tub with Fred and Michelle on either side of him.

"Hey, make room, you're crowding me," said Fred.

"Maybe we should hang out here for a while," said Michelle. David laughed but then he listened. He could hear his parents coming up the stairs.

He scrambled out of the tub, dried off hurriedly with a towel and then said goodbye to Fred and Michelle. There was a light tapping on the door and David heard his mother, "David, are you OK?"

"Yes, Mom, I'm just going to the bathroom."

"All right, wash your hands when you're done and I'll make you some breakfast."

He heard her walk away from the door, calling, "Cutie, Spud, breakfast."

Oh no, I left the cats in Remin, David thought in horror. How are they going to get back?

"Uh oh, looks like we screwed up!"

David turned and found Fred and Michelle looking up at him. Without even thinking he reached into his pocket for his wand. "That won't work here," said Fred sadly.

"We'll talk to Houdin when we get back. He'll find some way to get them back," said Michelle.

But David wasn't listening. He imagined a door that opened in Remin. He traced the door with his wand and thought about returning to Remin to get his cats. The wand suddenly grew warm and lines of light exploded in front of his eyes in the shape of a door. He turned and locked the bathroom door and while Fred and Michelle watched in amazement, he put his hand on the area outlined by the lines of light, stepped through the door, and vanished.

16 * PLEASANT DREAMS

He was falling through a vortex again and for one scary moment he thought he had made a mistake. He didn't understand how he had been able to make a door, or open it and step through it. The only thing that he was sure of was his own imagination, so he concentrated on the fountain and the Imaginator dome. Maybe the Imaginator had done something unexpected. Maybe it was leftover magic and this was the last thing he would be able to do. He didn't know but at least he would get his cats back.

He was standing in midair looking down a long tunnel. Behind him he could see the bathroom door. He concentrated on the tunnel in front of him and imagined the Remin plaza. The air was swirling around him, and as he focused on the picture in his mind a door lined in light appeared in front of him. He opened it and stepped through it . . . and found himself on his knees in the middle of the Remin plaza. His door was a foot off the ground and he stumbled as he stepped through it. *I obviously need some practice,* he thought happily. The plaza was empty, and the sun that had been high in the sky only moments ago was now sinking into sunset. David stood there, confused for a moment and then it came to him. Time moved faster here.

He turned and saw the dome of the Imaginator humming in the distance, and gliding around it was a mano guard that could only be Aradel. David grinned, called out, "Hey Aradel," and watched as Aradel stopped, looked over and waved heartily.

"Back so soon?" Aradel shouted.

David laughed, "I forgot my cats." He moved quickly toward Houdin's street.

Minutes later he was on the steps of Houdin's house and pushing the stars on the door. The familiar face swiveled into view. "Welcome to Houdin's house, how may I help you?" the face intoned without even looking up.

"Well, you could start by saying you missed me," David said.

The eyes on the face snapped open and the face broke into a large grin. "I didn't think I would see you again. Yes, I did miss you. Houdin doesn't pay as much attention to me. I assume you are here for your cats."

"Yes, how did you know?"

"Well, they've been meowing on the other side of this door since you left. I let them out and then they want to come back in. I let them in and they want to go back out. I can't figure out what they want. It's getting a little annoying." As the face said this, the door swung open and two furry blurs leaped into David's arms. Cutie and Spud set up a loud battle of purring, rubbing against his chin and licking his face. David felt their comforting warmth and stepped into the wizard's house.

Houdin met him in the hallway with a puzzled look on his face. "David, I am glad to see you and your cats certainly look happy, but I don't understand. Fred and Michelle were just telling me a fantastic story about how you used magic in your own world to open a portal to Remin. Is this true?"

"Yes!" David said with a big grin. "I just imagined the door and drew it with my wand and voila, the door appeared. I opened it and stepped through and here I am." He finished with a flourish of his hands setting off a mad scramble by both cats to stay perched in his arms.

Houdin shook his head and stepped into the study. David followed. The face popped up on the wall to watch as

Houdin walked behind his desk and began pulling down dusty books and leafing through them. He obviously didn't find what he was looking for because after a few minutes of rapidly turning pages he slammed a book shut with a resounding clap that filled the air with dust and turned back to the shelf. He picked up the glass ball with the pink lightning from the shelf and set it on his desk. He placed his own hands on the ball without any discernible effect. The lightning continued on its erratic path from the center of the ball to the glass.

Houdin removed his hands, dipped them into a spectrum sack and sprinkled the glass with red spectrum. He placed his hands back on the glass while David watched intently. As the aged wizard began murmuring a spell the lightning grew more intense and began seeking out the wizards fingertips. Soon all of the lightning bolts were crackling on Houdin's fingers, and as he massaged his fingers over the glass the electricity followed his fingertips. Houdin watched intently for a few moments, then broke the spell and carefully cleaned the glass with the edge of his robe. He pushed the lightning globe across the desk toward David.

"I want to test you with this globe. It won't hurt you. Place your wand on the desk, think about what you saw me do and then place your hands on the globe." His eyes were focusing intensely on the boy who now sat confidently across from him.

David placed the image in his mind of the lightning bolts under the control of his fingertips. Once he was sure he was correctly focused, he reached out with his hands and placed his fingers on opposite sides of the globe. Even as his fingers were approaching the glass the streams of light inside began seeking out his hands. When his fingers touched the glass all the bolts of lightning leaped to his fingertips as if they were metal and his fingers were magnets. David grinned and gently swirled his fingers over the glass, watching the pink bolts of energy follow his movements.

Houdin's mouth dropped open in amazement. "Extraordinary! That shouldn't be possible. The globe should only react that way to someone born in Remin."

The face swiveled out of view and returned moments later with Kira, who burst into the room, out of breath but completely healed. She scooped David up in a big bear hug. "So it's true. Aradel said you were back. I'm so glad to see you again. I wasn't sure we would ever meet again and certainly I didn't expect to see you so soon." She was squeezing him so hard that David finally let out a strangled hello and she released him. She turned to Houdin with a questioning glance.

Houdin shrugged. "I can't explain it. David was able to use magic outside of Remin. Only a wizard born in Remin should be able to do that. He opened a portal to Remin from his own world and came here to retrieve his cats."

Kira turned to David with a huge Cheshire cat grin. "I told you that you could be a wizard like Houdin. It looks like I was right." She paused for a few moments, thinking. "It must have something to do with his long exposure to the full power of the Imaginator this morning in the dome."

"Yes, yes, that much is obvious but what does it mean?" said Houdin impatiently. "I can't explain it without months or maybe years of analysis. Maybe it's a temporary effect that will wear off in a couple of days or maybe David is permanently altered into a magical David."

David, who had been listening closely to the discussion, now became ecstatic and began talking very fast. "That's it! I've always imagined that I could be magical. In the dome I thought about it and pictured myself protected from the harmful effects of the spectrum stone. It must have worked!" He began dancing around the room using the wand like a marching band baton and singing, "I have come to save the day. I am magical David. Nothing can stand in my way, I am magical David."

Houdin and Kira stared doubtfully at the cavorting boy. "It might not last, David."

"I don't believe that. And even if it doesn't last forever, I'm magical David right now and that's all right with me." He scooped up the cats and whirled around gleefully. "I've got to get back—my parents will wonder what is taking me so long."

Houdin reached into his pocket. "You dropped this during your transformation this morning." He held out the healing amulet. David watched the torchlight reflecting off the central stone, still black from Kira's ordeal, as he took it carefully and put it around his neck.

David turned to the face on the wall. "Goodbye, I'll miss you, but I'll be back sometime soon." The face began crying. David patted it on the head and as the face continued to sniffle, he traced a door with his wand. The glimmering lines of light appeared in midair again. David concentrated on the bathroom in his house, waved to Houdin and Kira who were just now beginning to grin, and stepped into the doorway. His leg vanished as he stepped in. "Really, I'll be back soon." Still smiling, he stepped forward and vanished from Kira and Houdin's sight.

The journey back was much easier. David found that he could easily stay focused on the goal. Moments later he stepped out of thin air and reappeared in his bathroom, still holding the cats. His mother was rapping frantically on the door.

"David, are you OK? Answer me!"

"I'm fine Mom, I was just daydreaming." David giggled to himself. That's not far from the truth, he thought.

His mother sounded relieved. "Have you seen the cats? I can't find them anywhere."

"They're right here with me." David glanced at the cats, which began meowing loudly.

"Well, hurry up, breakfast is ready."

"OK, mom."

David opened the bathroom door and went back to his room. He put his dirty clothes in the hamper and then removed the healing amulet and placed it in his treasure box. He placed his wand under his pillow and headed to the dining room for breakfast.

His father was sitting at the breakfast table, reading the newspaper. David bounced into the room and ran up to his dad. "Guess what?"

His father sighed and lowered his paper. "What?"

"I'm really magical David!"

"That's nice."

"No, really!"

"Well if you are, I wouldn't spread that around or everyone will want to be magical too." His father went back to his paper.

David knew that it was really unbelievable but he wanted them to know. "Mom, I have a great story to tell you. One of our caterpillars was really a wizard who was under a curse. I took him back to his world which is called Remin and…" His voice trailed off. His parents were both looking at him with amused expressions. At that moment he realized that they didn't believe and that maybe it was better that way. It would be his secret. Maybe one day he would show them but right now it was better to keep it to himself. He shrugged. "It's a really good story."

"I'm sure it is and I'd love to hear it. Let's talk about it after breakfast."

The whole adventure came flooding back to him and suddenly David felt very tired. "I'm not hungry. I'm tired. I'm going to take a nap."

His mother looked concerned. "Are you feeling OK?"

"I'm fine. I'm just tired."

His father and mother both walked back to his bedroom with him. He climbed under the covers and curled up. He put his hand under his pillow and felt the comforting shape of his wand.

"Did you sleep well last night?" his father asked.

"Not really."

"Nightmares again?"

"Sort of."

"Well, take a little nap. Mommy and Daddy both hope you have good dreams."

Magical David smiled up at them. "Oh, I'm sure I will."

As they turned to leave his mother stopped, "Oh where did you find this chrysalis? Your caterpillars are just hatching out." She was pointing at an empty chrysalis sitting all alone on a shelf.

David looked sheepish and shrugged, and his parents walked out of the room with slightly puzzled expressions on their faces, forgetting that the light was still on. Magical David grinned, glanced at the light switch, aimed his wand and watched the switch turn off all by itself. The sunlight filtered through the window and reflected on the golden lines on the chrysalis and a few tiny sparkles of glitter. He smiled and closed his eyes, and for the first time in a long time, slipped into a deep sleep filled with pleasant dreams.

If you enjoyed this book, share it with a friend!

For more Remin fun, visit the Dark Dreamweaver website at:
www.DarkDreamweaver.com

I'd love to hear from you.
If you'd like to write me a letter, you can send it to:

Nick Ruth
c/o Imaginator Press
6400 Baltimore Nat'l Pike #194
Baltimore, MD 21228-3915

FIND HOUDIN

FIND HOUDIN

So, you want to find your own Monarch caterpillar wizard? This section is loaded with information that can help you find the Monarch in any stage of its lifecycle. If you live in the United States, you have a good chance of finding this amazing insect. I can't guarantee that it will talk to you, or propel you on an adventure to another world, but you never know.

MILKWEED

Why am I telling you about a weed? The best place to begin looking for the Monarch is on and around this plant. Milkweed is the host plant for the Monarch, and it spends a good part of its life on the Milkweed plant.

Did you ever find a caterpillar and put it in a jar with some leaves, only to find out that it wouldn't eat the leaves you gave it? Most caterpillars are very picky eaters. Each species of caterpillar will only eat leaves of certain types. In the case of the Monarch caterpillar, it will only eat leaves of the milkweed plant.

How can you find the milkweed plant? The best place to look is in open fields, abandoned lots, and along the sides of roads. Usually it is one of the tallest plants in the field, towering over the other vegetation. If you break off a leaf from a milk-weed plant, it bleeds a milky, sticky sap.

LIFECYCLE OF THE MONARCH

The eggs of the Monarch are tiny, white and football shaped. They are no bigger than the head of a pin, but they don't look like a pinhead! They have a definite point on top, and ridges radiate down the egg from the point. Monarch eggs are usually found on the underside of milkweed leaves, near the top of the plant.

When the eggs first hatch, the caterpillars are, as in the story, no bigger than a grain of rice. At this first stage they are green and do not yet have any stripes. After a few days, yellow and black stripes begin to appear. As they grow, they molt, or shed their skin, enabling them to grow larger. You will rarely see this discarded skin, as the caterpillar usually eats it. (Yuck!)

You may have been told that caterpillars spin a cocoon to turn into a butterfly. If so, you were told incorrectly! Butterfly caterpillars do not spin cocoons. If you see a cater-pillar spinning a cocoon, chances are it is going to become a moth, not a butterfly. Butterfly caterpillars actually transform themselves into an intermediate stage called a chrysalis (sci-entists call this the pupa). This transformation is amazing to watch! When the Monarch caterpillar is ready to become a chrysalis, it hangs upside down in the shape of the letter J. It wiggles around for several hours, until finally its skin splits and the chrysalis emerges where the caterpillar used to be. Now that's real magic!

Initially, the chrysalis is soft and wiggles around quite a bit, but within a few hours it hardens into a beautiful green and gold jewel. To your eye, the chrysalis appears to be just hang-ing around, doing nothing, but inside the skin it is actually undergoing its final transformation into a butterfly. Towards the end of this period, you will begin to see the orange and black wing patterns through the skin of the chrysalis.

When the butterfly is ready, the skin of the chrysalis splits and the butterfly emerges, leaving an empty chrysalis. When the butterfly first emerges, its wings are wet, so it hangs upside-down from the chrysalis until the wings dry.

It takes about a month for a Monarch to go from egg to butterfly. In the story, Houdin passes through each stage much more quickly because his lifecycle is speeded up by the time difference between Remin and our world.

THE MIGRATION

Like birds flying south for the winter, the Monarchs migrate south every year when the weather gets colder and the days get shorter. Every winter, the eastern Monarchs migrate to central Mexico and the western Monarchs migrate to California, where they spend the winter. In the spring, they begin to migrate north again. Butterflies live fairly short lives, so most of the butterflies that go north don't live long enough to make the journey back south again. They lay eggs along the way and their children continue the journey where they left off. I sometimes get lost in my neighborhood, yet somehow these butterflies know exactly where to go, even though they've never been there before.

FOR MORE INFORMATION

If you'd like to learn more, or maybe try your hand at butterfly gardening or raising Monarchs, the following web sites are a great place to go for more information:

Monarch Watch
http://www.monarchwatch.org/
Monarch Watch began as a research project and evolved into much more. At this site you will find lots of articles about Monarch biology, raising Monarchs,

and butterfly gardening. You can order a tagging kit and tag butterflies to participate in the migration study. Monarch Watch also sells many other Monarch related items, including butterfly gardening kits and Monarch rearing kits.

Journey North
http://www.learner.org/jnorth/
Journey North studies the northward migration of a number of animals, including the Monarch. The have lots of excellent information about the Monarch. They also plot sightings of the Monarchs during the northward migration on a map, which you can view at the web site. You can even report your own sightings!

For more Monarch information and links, please visit www.DarkDreamweaver.com

ACKNOWLEDGMENTS

I t's a rare book indeed that springs from the author's mind and makes it to the printed page unassisted. This book is not rare, and so there are many people that deserve thanks for making *The Dark Dreamweaver* a reality.

First and foremost, my wife Sheila, who, after getting over her astonishment that I could actually write an imaginative story, plunged into the murky world of publishing and spent countless hours to get these pages into your hands. Her enthusiasm for the story and her helpful criticism smoothed out the rough spots and improved my initial ideas.

My mother-in-law, Edna French, who contributed her extensive literary editing skills to numerous drafts. Aradel's coat would still be lost if not for her, and Houdin would be a fairly boring wizard without her input.

Sue Concannon, who brought the world of Remin to life. If a picture is worth a thousand words, then this story is 18,000 words better than I could have dreamed, even though she still thinks Thane looks fat in Chapter 1.

Sue's husband, Tom Concannon, who got into the spirit of the book and helped come up with ideas for some of the images you see here.

Vicky Al-Toukhi, who got so enthused about the story she made extensive notes and comments on early drafts and helped to fix some glaring mistakes. She thinks the "Wrestle Fight" would make a great game, but heck if I can figure out how.

Dalal Al-Toukhi, just for making my day job easier.

Danny Kotowski for staying up late reading the initial draft. The first enthusiastic reader who convinced me that it might be nice to share this story with others.

Andi Buchanan, for typesetting and designing the book. She pulled it all together and made it look like a real book.

The Transparent Sands craft booth at the Maryland Renaissance Festival for designing the wand that was the inspiration for "spectrum power."

And last, but certainly not least, my entire family, who support me in whatever I do, even if it's not very good. I certainly hope that's not the case here. Thanks, Mom, Dad, Anne, Joan, George, Bill, Kasey, Jessie, Nikki, and Rachel.